Thomas Buchanan Read

# Poems

Thomas Buchanan Read

**Poems**

ISBN/EAN: 9783743382664

Manufactured in Europe, USA, Canada, Australia, Japa

Cover: Foto ©Andreas Hilbeck / pixelio.de

Manufactured and distributed by brebook publishing software (www.brebook.com)

Thomas Buchanan Read

**Poems**

# POEMS

BY

## THOMAS BUCHANAN READ.

A NEW AND ENLARGED EDITION.

IN TWO VOLUMES.

VOL. I.

PHILADELPHIA:

J. B. LIPPINCOTT & CO

1866.

Entered according to Act of Congress, in the year 1859, by

THOMAS BUCHANAN READ,

in the Clerk's Office of the District Court of the District of Massachusetts.

TO

JOHN A. C. GRAY, Esq.,

AS AN EVIDENCE OF SINCERE REGARD

These Poems

ARE INSCRIBED BY

THE AUTHOR.

# CONTENTS OF VOL. I.

## LYRIC POEMS.

# CONTENTS. vii

## SYLVIA; OR, THE LAST SHEPHERD.



## MISCELLANEOUS.

.

# AIRS FROM ALPLAND.

# LYRIC POEMS.

# MY HERMITAGE.

Within a wood, one summer's day,
  And in a hollow, ancient trunk,
I shut me from the world away,
  To live as lives a hermit monk.

My cell a ghostly sycamore,
  The roots and boughs were dead with age;
Decay had carved the gothic door
  Which looked into my hermitage.

My library was large and full,
  Where, ever as a hermit plods,
I read until my eyes were dull
  With tears; for all those tomes were God's.

The vine that at my doorway swung
Had verses writ on every leaf,
The very songs the bright bees sung
In honey-seeking visits brief—

Not brief—though each stayed never long—
So rapidly they came and went
No pause was left in all their song,
For while they borrowed still they lent.

All day the woodland minstrels sang—
Small feet were in the leaves astir—
And often o'er my doorway rang
The tap of a blue-winged visiter.

Afar the stately river swayed,
And poured itself in giant swells,
While here the brooklet danced and played,
And gayly rung its liquid bells.

The springs gave me their crystal flood,
And my contentment made it wine—
And oft I found what kingly food
Grew on the world-forgotten vine.

The moss, or weed, or running flower,
   Too humble in their hope to climb,
Had in themselves the lovely power
   To make me happier for the time.


And when the starry night came by,
   And stooping looked into my cell,
Then all between the earth and sky
   Was circled in a holier spell.


A height, and depth, and breadth sublime
   O'erspread the scene, and reached the stars,
Until Eternity and Time
   Seemed drowning their dividing bars.


And voices which the day ne'er hears,
   And visions which the sun ne'er sees,
From earth and from the distant spheres,
   Came on the moonlight and the breeze.


Thus day and night my spirit grew
   In love with that which round me shone,
Until my calm heart fully knew
   The joy it is to be alone.

The time went by—till one fair dawn
   I saw against the eastern fires
A visionary city drawn,
   With dusky lines of domes and spires.


The wind in sad and fitful spells
   Blew o'er it from the gates of morn,
Till I could clearly hear the bells
   That rung above a world forlorn.


And well I listened to their voice,
   And deeply pondered what they said—
Till I arose—there was no choice—
   I went while yet the east was red.


My wakened heart for utterance yearned—
   The clamorous wind had broke the spell—
I needs must teach what I had learned
   Within my simple woodland cell.

# AN INVITATION.



Come thou, my friend;—the cool autumnal eves
  About the hearth have drawn their magic rings;
There, while his song of peace the cricket weaves,
  The simmering hickory sings.


The winds unkennelled round the casements whine,
  The sheltered hound makes answer in his dream,
And in the hayloft, hark, the cock at nine,
  Crows from the dusty beam.
  2

The leafless branches chafe the roof all night,
 And through the house the troubled noises go,
While, like a ghostly presence, thin and white,
 The frost foretells the snow.


The muffled owl within the swaying elm
 Thrills all the air with sadness as he swings,
Till sorrow seems to spread her shadowy realm
 About all outward things.


Come, then, my friend, and this shall seem no more—
 Come when October walks his red domain,
Or when November from his windy floor
 Winnows the hail and rain:


And when old Winter through his fingers numb
 Blows till his breathings on the windows gleam;
And when the mill-wheel spiked with ice is dumb
 Within the neighbouring stream:


Then come, for nights like these have power to wake
 The calm delight no others may impart,
When round the fire true souls communing make
 A summer in the heart.

And I will weave athwart the mystic gloom,
   With hand grown weird in strange romance, for thee,
Bright webs of fancy from the golden loom
   Of charmèd Poesy.


And let no censure in thy looks be shown,
   That I, with hands adventurous and bold,
Should grasp the enchanted shuttle which was thrown
   Through mightier warps of old.

# A SONG.

Bring me the juice of the honey fruit,
　The large translucent, amber-hued,
Rare grapes of southern isles, to suit
　The luxury that fills my mood.

And bring me only such as grew
　Where fairest maidens tend the bowers,
And only fed by rain and dew
　Which first had bathed a bank of flowers.

They must have hung on spicy trees
  In airs of far enchanted vales,
And all night heard the ecstasies
  Of noble-throated nightingales :


So that the virtues which belong
  To flowers may therein tasted be,
And that which hath been thrilled with song
  May give a thrill of song to me.


For I would wake that string for thee
  Which hath too long in silence hung,
And sweeter than all else should be
  The song which in thy praise is sung.

# THE DESERTED ROAD.

Ancient road, that wind'st deserted
　　Through the level of the vale,
Sweeping toward the crowded market
　　Like a stream without a sail;

Standing by thee, I look backward,
　　And, as in the light of dreams,
See the years descend and vanish,
　　Like thy tented wains and teams.

Here I stroll along the village
   As in youth's departed morn;
But I miss the crowded coaches,
   And the driver's bugle-horn—

Miss the crowd of jovial teamsters
   Filling buckets at the wells,
With their wains from Conestoga,
   And their orchestras of bells.

To the mossy way-side tavern
   Comes the noisy throng no more,
And the faded sign, complaining,
   Swings, unnoticed, at the door;

While the old, decrepid tollman,
   Waiting for the few who pass,
Reads the melancholy story
   In the thickly springing grass.

Ancient highway, thou art vanquished
   The usurper of the vale
Rolls in fiery, iron rattle,
   Exultations on the gale.

Thou art vanquished and neglected;
But the good which thou hast done
Though by man it be forgotten,
Shall be deathless as the sun.


Though neglected, gray and grassy,
Still I pray that my decline
May be through as vernal valleys
And as blest a calm as thine.

# A BUTTERFLY IN THE CITY.

Dear transient spirit of the fields,
　　Thou com'st without distrust,
To fan the sunshine of our streets
　　Among the noise and dust.

Thou leadest in thy wavering flight
　　My footsteps unaware,
Until I seem to walk the vales
　　And breathe thy native air.

And thou hast fed upon the flowers,
  And drained their honeyed springs,
Till every tender hue they wore
  Is blooming on thy wings.


I bless the fresh and flowery light
  Thou bringest to the town,
But tremble lest the hot turmoil
  Have power to weigh thee down;


For thou art like the poet's song,
  Arrayed in holiest dyes,
Though it hath drained the honeyed wells
  Of flowers of Paradise,


Though it hath brought celestial hues
  To light the ways of life,
The dust shall weigh its pinions down
  Amid the noisy strife.


And yet, perchance, some kindred soul
  May see its glory shine,
And feel its wings within his heart
  As bright as I do thine.

# THE WAY-SIDE SPRING.

Fair dweller by the dusty way—
  Bright saint within a mossy shrine,
The tribute of a heart to-day
  Weary and worn is thine.


The earliest blossoms of the year,
  The sweet-briar and the violet
The pious hand of Spring has here
  Upon thy altar set.

And not alone to thee is given
　　The homage of the pilgrim's knee—
But oft the sweetest birds of Heaven
　　Glide down and sing to thee.


Here daily from his beechen cell
　　The hermit squirrel steals to drink,
And flocks which cluster to their bell
　　Recline along thy brink.


And here the wagoner blocks his wheels,
　　To quaff the cool and generous boon;
Here from the sultry harvest fields
　　The reapers rest at noon.


And oft the beggar masked with tan,
　　In rusty garments gray with dust,
Here sits and dips his little can,
　　And breaks his scanty crust;


And, lulled beside thy whispering stream,
　　Oft drops to slumber unawares,
And sees the angel of his dream
　　Upon celestial stairs.

Dear dweller by the dusty way,
  Thou saint within a mossy shrine,
The tribute of a heart to-day
  Weary and worn is thine!

# A MAYING.

## PART FIRST.

Now sitting under orchard limbs,
    When all the world has gone a-Maying,
Oh, how the fancy soars and skims,
    With yonder fitful swallow playing !

Like snowy tents, the trees in bloom
    Stand courting every bee that's winging ;
And in the depths of their perfume
    A whole community is singing.

The wind upon these murmuring bowers,
    From out the fields of clover blowing,
Shakes down a storm of scented flowers,
    As if to fright me with its snowing.

The blue-bird, which from Southern skies
  Takes yearly on his wings their azure,
Now through the falling blossoms flies,
  And thrills the passing air with pleasure.


Oh, would that I could thus take flight,
  And be, like him, the earliest comer,
That all should hear me with delight,
  And bless the song that promised summer !


Along the quiet, neighbouring town,
  The children chant their gladsome marches;
Each with a woodland gathered crown,—
  Some under flowery iris-arches.


Afar and near the music swells—
  The breeze is glad to waft their singing,
For never chime of fairy bells
  Filled poet's soul with sweeter ringing.


See where they go !—a very cloud
  With rosy pleasure overladen !
Sure Flora hath to-day endowed
  With her own form each little maiden.

A gladness thrills the waiting grove
　　While they go singing gayly over;—
The very fields are waked to love,
　　And nod them welcome with the clover.


And every flower where stoops the breeze
　　With just enough of force to stir it,
Rings out its little chime of bees,
　　In pleasure from its vernal turret.


The springs release their fullest floods,
　　From earth's o'erflowing heart, unbidden.
The woodlands ope their latest buds,
　　There's not a leaf that may be hidden.


Yes, surely there's a love abroad,
　　Through every nerve of nature playing,—
And all between the sky and sod,
　　All, all the world has gone a-Maying!


## SECOND PART.

Oh, wherefore do I sit and give
　　My Fancy up to idle playing?

Too well I know the half who live—
    One-half the world is NOT a-Maying.


Where are the dwellers of the lanes,
    The alleys of the stifled city?
Where the waste forms whose sad remains
    Woo Death to come for very pity?


Where they who tend the busy loom,
    With pallid cheek and torn apparel?
The buds they weave will never bloom,
    Their staring birds will never carol.


It may be at the thought, their souls
    Are crushed to-day in their abasement,—
Oh, better they should house with owls,
    With poison vines about their casement!


And where the young of every size
    The factories draw from every by-way,
Whose violets are each other's eyes,
    But dull as by a dusty highway?—

Whose cotton lilies only grow
   'Mid whirring wheels, on jarring spindles,
Their roses in the hectic glow
   To tell how fast the small life dwindles?

Or she who plies the midnight thread
   The while her orphan ones are sleeping,
And trembles lest, for want of bread,
   They start from troubled dreams to weeping?

Not all the floral wealth that sweeps
   The brow of May in splendour shining,
Were worth to her the crust that keeps
   Her little ones to-day from pining.

Where are the dusky miners? they
   Who, even in the earth descending,
Know well the night before their May
   Is one which has in life no ending?

To them 'tis still a joy, I ween,
   To know, while through the darkness going,
That o'er their heads the smiling queen
   Stands with her countless garlands glowing.

Oh, ye who toil in living tombs
    Of light or dark—no rest receiving,
Far o'er your heads a May-time blooms—
    Oh, then be patient and believing.


Be patient—when Earth's winter fails,
    The weary night which keeps ye staying—
Then through the broad celestial vales
    Your spirits shall go out a-Maying!

# THE SUMMER SHOWER.

BEFORE the stout harvesters falleth the grain,
As when the strong storm-wind is reaping the plain;
And loiters the boy in the briery lane;
But yonder aslant comes the silvery rain,
Like a long line of spears brightly burnished and tall.

Adown the white highway, like cavalry fleet,
It dashes the dust with its numberless feet.
Like a murmurless school, in their leafy retreat,
The wild birds sit listening the drops round them beat;
And the boy crouches close to the blackberry wall.

The swallows alone take the storm on their wing,
And, taunting the tree-sheltered labourers, sing.
Like pebbles the rain breaks the face of the spring,
While a bubble darts up from each widening ring;
And the boy, in dismay, hears the loud shower fall.

But soon are the harvesters tossing the sheaves;
The robin darts out from its bower of leaves;
The wren peereth forth from the moss-covered eaves;
And the rain-spattered urchin now gladly perceives
That the beautiful bow bendeth over them all.

# INEZ.

Down behind the hidden village, fringed around with
    hazel brake,
(Like a holy hermit dreaming, half asleep and half
    awake,
One who loveth the sweet quiet for the happy quiet's
    sake,)
Dozing, murmuring in its visions, lay the heaven-ena-
    moured lake.


And within a dell, where shadows through the brightest
    days abide,
Like the silvery swimming gossamer by breezes scat-
    tered wide,
Fell a shining skein of water that ran down the lakelet's
    side,
As within the brain by beauty lulled, a pleasant thought
    may glide.

When the sinking sun of August, growing large in the
    decline,
Shot his arrows long and golden through the maple and
    the pine;
And the russet-thrush fled singing from the alder to the
    vine,
While the cat-bird in the hazel gave its melancholy
    whine;


And the little squirrel chattered, peering round the
    hickory bole,
And, a-sudden like a meteor, gleamed along the
    oriole;—
There I walked beside fair Inez, and her gentle beauty
    stole
Like the scene athwart my senses, like the sunshine
    through my soul.


And her fairy feet that pressed the leaves, a pleasant
    music made,
And they dimpled the sweet beds of moss with blossoms
    thick inlaid:—

There I told her old romances, and with love's sweet woe
    we played,
Till fair Inez' eyes, like evening, held the dew beneath
    their shade.


There I wove for her love ballads, such as lover only
    weaves,
Till she sighed and grieved, as only mild and loving
    maiden grieves;
And to hide her tears she stooped to glean the violets
    from the leaves,
As of old sweet Ruth went gleaning 'mid the oriental
    sheaves.


Down we walked beside the lakelet:—gazing deep into
    her eye,
There I told her all my passion!  With a sudden blush
    and sigh,
Turning half away with look askant, she only made
    reply,
" How deep within the water glows the happy evening
    sky !"

Then I asked her if she loved me, and our hands met
    each in each,
And the dainty, sighing ripples seemed to listen up the
    reach;
While thus slowly with a hazel wand she wrote along
    the beach,
" Love, like the sky, lies deepest ere the heart is stirred
    to speech."


Thus I gained the love of Inez—thus I won her gentle
    hand;
And our paths now lie together, as our footprints on the
    strand;
We have vowed to love each other in the golden morn-
    ing land,
When our names from earth have vanished, like the
    writing from the sand!

# SUNLIGHT ON THE THRESHOLD.

Dear Mary, I remember yet
  The day when first we rode together,
Through groves where grew the violet,
  For it was in the Maying weather.


And I remember how the woods
  Were thrilled with love's delightful chorus;
How in the scented air the buds,
  Like our young hearts, were swelling o'er us.


The little birds, in tuneful play,
  Along the fence before us fluttered;
The robin hopped across the way,
  Then turned to hear the words we uttered!

We stopped beside the willow-brook,
  That trickled through its bed of rushes;
While timidly the reins you took,
  I gathered blooms from briar bushes;


And one I placed, with fingers meek,
  Within your little airy bonnet;
But then I looked and saw your cheek—
  Another rose was blooming on it!


Some miles beyond the village lay,
  Where pleasures were in wait to wreathe us;
While swiftly flew the hours away,
  As swiftly flew the road beneath us


How gladly we beheld arise,
  Across the hill, the village steeple;
Then met the urchin's wondering eyes,
  And gaze of window-peering people!


The dusty coach that brought the mail,
  Before the office-door was standing;
Beyond, the blacksmith, gray and hale,
  With burning tire the wheel was banding.

We passed some fruit-trees—after these
 A bedded garden lying sunward;
Then saw, beneath three aged trees,
 The parsonage a little onward.


A modest building, somewhat gray,
 Escaped from time, from storm, disaster;
The very threshold worn away
 With feet of those who'd sought the pastor.


And standing on the threshold there,
 We saw a child of angel lightness;
Her soul-lit face—her form of air,
 Outshone the sunlight with their brightness!


As then she stood I see her now—
 In years perchance a half a dozen—
And Mary, you remember how
 She ran to you and called you "cousin?"


As then, I see her slender size,
 Her flowing locks upon her shoulder—
A six years' loss to Paradise,
 And ne'er on earth the child grew older!

Thrce times the flowers have dropped away,
   Three winters glided gayly o'er us,
Since here upon that morn in May
   The little maiden stood before us.

These are the elms, and this the door,
   With trailing woodbine overshaded;
But from the step, for evermore,
   The sunlight of that child has faded!

# MIDNIGHT.

The moon looks down on a world of snow,
And the midnight lamp is burning low,
And the fading embers mildly glow
In their bed of ashes soft and deep;
All, all is still as the hour of death;
I only hear what the old clock saith,
And the mother and infant's easy breath,
That flows from the holy land of Sleep.

Say on, old clock—I love you well,
For your silver chime, and the truths you tell,
Your every stroke is but the knell
Of hope, or sorrow buried deep;
Say on—but only let me hear
The sound most sweet to my listening ear,
The child and the mother breathing clear
Within the harvest-fields of Sleep.

Thou watchman, on thy lonely round,
I thank thee for that warning sound;
The clarion cock and the baying hound
  Not less their dreary vigils keep;
Still hearkening, I will love you all,
While in each silent interval
I hear those dear breasts rise and fall
  Upon the airy tide of Sleep.


Old world, on time's benighted stream
Sweep down till the stars of morning beam
From orient shores—nor break the dream
  That calms my love to pleasure deep;
Roll on, and give my Bud and Rose
The fulness of thy best repose,
The blessedness which only flows
  Along the silent realms of Sleep.

# THE LIGHT OF OUR HOME.

Oh, thou whose beauty on us beams
　　With glimpses of celestial light;
Thou halo of our waking dreams,
　　And early star that crown'st our night;

Thy light is magic where it falls;
　　To thee the deepest shadow yields;
Thou bring'st unto these dreary halls
　　The lustre of the summer-fields.

There is a freedom in thy looks
  To make the prisoned heart rejoice ;—
In thy blue eyes I see the brooks,
  And hear their music in thy voice.


And every sweetest bird that sings
  Hath poured a charm upon thy tongue;
And where the bee enamoured clings,
  There surely thou in love hast clung :—


For when I hear thy laughter free,
  And see thy morning-lighted hair,
As in a dream at once I see
  Fair upland realms and valleys fair.


I see thy feet empearled with dews,
  The violet's and the lily's loss;
And where the waving woodland woos
  Thou lead'st me over beds of moss ;—


And by the busy runnel's side,
  Whose waters, like a bird afraid,
Dart from their fount, and flashing, glide
  Athwart the sunshine and the shade.

Or larger streams our steps beguile ;—·
  We see the cascade, broad and fair,
Dashed headlong down to foam, the while
  Its iris-spirit leaps to air !


Alas ! as by a loud alarm,
  The fancied turmoil of the falls
Hath driven me back and broke the charm
  Which led me from these alien walls :—


Yes, alien, dearest child, are these
  Close city walls to thee and me :
My homestead was embowered with trees,
  And such thy heritage should be :—


And shall be ;—I will make for thee
  A home within my native vale,
Where every brook and ancient tree
  Shall whisper some long-treasured tale.


Now once again I see thee stand,
  As down the future years I gaze,
The fairest maiden of the land,
  The spirit of those sylvan ways.

And in thy looks again I trace
  The light of her who gave thee birth;
She who endowed thy form and face
  With glory which is not of Earth.


And as I gaze upon her now,
  My heart sends up a prayer for thee,
That thou mayest wear upon thy brow
  The light which now she beams on me.

# THE TWO DOVES.

When the Spring's delightful store
　　Brought the blue-birds to our bowers,
And the poplar at the door
　　Shook the fragrance from its flowers,
Then there came two wedded doves,
　　And they built among the limbs,
And the murmur of their loves
　　Fell like mellow, distant hymns;
There, until the Spring had flown,
　　Did they sit and sing alone,
In the broad and flowery branches.

With the scented Summer breeze
  How their music swam around,
Till my spirit sailed the seas
  Of enchanted realms of sound!
"Soul," said I, "thy dream of youth
  Is not fancy, nor deceives,
For I hear Love's blissful truth
  Prophesied among the leaves;
Therefore till the Summer's flown
  Sit and sing, but not alone,
In the broad and flowery branches."


Then the harvest came and went,
  And the Autumn marshalled down
All his host, and spread his tent
  Over fields and forests brown;
Then the doves, one evening, hied
  To their old accustomed nest;
One went up, but drooped and died,
  With an arrow in its breast—
Died and dropped; while there, alone,
  Sat the other, making moan,
In the broad and withering branches.

There it sat and mourned its mate,
  With a never-ending moan,
Till I thought perchance its fate
  Was prophetic of my own:
And at each lament I heard,
  How the tears sprang to my eyes!
O! I could have clasped the bird,
  And communed with it in sighs;
But it drooped—and with a moan,
  Closed its eyes, and there, alone,
Dropped from out the leafless branches.


I beheld it on the ground,
  Press the brown leaves, cold and dead,
And my brain went round and round,
  And I clasped my throbbing head,
While thus spake a voice of Love:
  " Rise, thou timid spirit, rise!
Earth has claimed the fallen dove—
  But thy soul shall cleave the skies;
While the angel, earlier flown,
  Shall sit waiting thee, alone,
In the green eternal branches!"

# SOLEMN VOICES.

I HEARD from out the dreary realms of Sorrow
　　The various tongues of Woe :—
One said, "Is there a hope in the to-morrow?"
　　And many answered, "No!"


And they arose and mingled their loud voices,
　　And cried in bitter breath,
"In all our joys the Past alone rejoices,—
　　There is no joy but Death.


"Oh dreadful Past, beyond thy midnight portal
　　Thou hast usurped our peace;
And if the angel Memory be immortal,
　　When shall this anguish cease?"

And suddenly within the darkened distance
    The solemn Past replied,
"In my domains your joys have no existence,
    Your hopes they have not died!


"Nought comes to me except those ghosts detested
    Phantoms of Wrong and Pain;
But whatso'er Affection hath invested,
    Th' eternal years retain.


"Then stand no more with looks and souls dejected,
    To woo and win despair,
The joys ye mourn the Future hath collected,
    Your hopes are gathered there.


"And as the dew which leaves the morning flowers
    Augments the after rain,—
And as the blooms which fall from summer bowers,
    Are multiplied again,—


"So shall the joys the Future holds in keeping,
    Augment your after peace;
So shall your hopes, which now are only sleeping,
    Return with large increase."

# SOME THINGS LOVE ME.

ALL within and all without me
    Feel a melancholy thrill;
And the darkness hangs about me,
    Oh, how still;
To my feet, the river glideth
    Through the shadow, sullen, dark;
On the stream the white moon rideth,
    Like a barque—
And the linden leans above me,
    Till I think some things there be
In this dreary world that love me,
    Even me!

Gentle buds are blooming near me,
 Shedding sweetest breath around ;
Countless voices rise, to cheer me,
 From the ground ;
And the lone bird comes—I hear it
 In the tall and windy pine
Pour the sadness of its spirit
 Into mine ;
There it swings and sings above me,
 Till I think some things there be
In this dreary world that love me,
 Even me !


Now the moon hath floated to me,
 On the stream I see it sway,
Swinging, boat-like, as 't would woo me
 Far away—
And the stars bend from the azure,
 I could reach them where I lie,
And they whisper all the pleasure
 Of the sky.
There they hang and smile above me,
 Till I think some things there be
In the very heavens that love me,
 Even me !

# TO WORDSWORTH.

Thy rise was as the morning, glorious, bright!
And error vanished like the affrighted dark;—
While many a soul, as the aspiring lark,
Waked by thy dawn, soared singing to the light,
Drowning in gladdest song the earth's despite!
And beauty blossomed in all lowly nooks—
Love, like a river made of nameless brooks,
Grew and exulted in thy wakening sight!
All nature hailed thee as a risen sun;
Nor will thy setting blur her thankful eyes!
While earth remains thy day shall not be done,
Nor cloud dispread to blot thy matchless skies!
When Death's command, like Joshua's, shall arise,
Thou'lt stand as stood the sun of Gibeon!

# PASSING THE ICEBERGS.

A FEARLESS shape of brave device,
　　Our vessel drives through mist and rain,
Between the floating fleets of ice—
　　The navies of the northern main.


These arctic ventures, blindly hurled,
　　The proofs of Nature's olden force,—
Like fragments of a crystal world
　　Long shattered from its skiey course.


These are the buccaneers that fright
　　The middle sea with dream of wrecks,
And freeze the south winds in their flight,
　　And chain the Gulf-stream to their decks.

PASSING THE ICEBERGS.

At every dragon prow and helm
    There stands some Viking as of yore;
Grim heroes from the boreal realm
    Where Odin rules the spectral shore.


And oft beneath the sun or moon
    Their swift and eager falchions glow—
While, like a storm-vexed wind, the rune
    Comes chafing through some beard of snow.


And when the far North flashes up
    With fires of mingled red and gold,
They know that many a blazing cup
    Is brimming to the absent bold.


Up signal there, and let us hail
    Yon looming phantom as we pass!—
Note all her fashion, hull, and sail,
    Within the compass of your glass.


See at her mast the steadfast glow
    Of that one star of Odin's throne;
Up with our flag, and let us show
    The Constellation on our own.

And speak her well; for she might say,
  If from her heart the words could thaw,
Great news from some far frozen bay,
  Or the remotest Esquimaux.


Might tell of channels yet untold,
  That sweep the pole from sea to sea;
Of lands which God designs to hold
  A mighty people yet to be :—


Of wonders which alone prevail
  Where day and darkness dimly meet ;—
Of all which spreads the arctic sail ;
  Of Franklin and his venturous fleet :


How, haply, at some glorious goal
  His anchor holds—his sails are furled ;
That Fame has named him on her scroll,
  "Columbus of the Polar World."


Or how his ploughing barques wedge on
  Through splintering fields, with battered shares,
Lit only by that spectral dawn,
  The mask that mocking darkness wears ;—

Or how, o'er embers black and few,
  The last of shivered masts and spars,
He sits amid his frozen crew
  In council with the norland stars.


No answer—but the sullen flow
  Of ocean heaving long and vast;—
An argosy of ice and snow,
  The voiceless North swings proudly past.

# CHRISTINE.

*Supposed to be related by a young sculptor on the hill-side between Florence and Fiesolé.*

Come, my friend, and in the silence and the shadow
    wrapt apart,
I will loose the golden claspings of this sacred tome—
    the heart.


By the bole of yonder cedar, under branches spread
    like eaves,
We will sit where wavering sunshine weaves romance
    among the leaves.

There by gentle airs of story shall our dreamy minds be
swayed,
And our spirits hang vibrating like the sunshine with
the shade.


Thou shalt sit, and leaning o'er me, calmly look into
my heart,
Look as Fiesolé above us looketh on Val d'Arno's
mart :—


Shalt behold how Love's fair river down the golden
city goes,
As the silent stream of Arno through the streets of
Florence flows.


I was standing o'er the marble, in the twilight falling
gray,
All my hopes and all my courage waning from me like
the day:


There I leaned across the statue, heaving many a sigh
and groan,
For I deemed the world as heartless, aye, as heartless as
the stone !

5

Nay, I well nigh thought the marble was a portion of
　　my pain,
For it seemed a frozen sorrow just without my burning
　　brain.


Then a cold and deathlike stupor slowly crept along my
　　frame,
While my life seemed passing outward, like a pale
　　reluctant flame.


And my weary soul went from me, and it walked the
　　world alone,
O'er a wide and brazen desert, in a hot and brazen
　　zone;


There it walked and trailed its pinions, slowly trailed
　　them in the sands,
With its hopeless eyes fixed blindly with its hopeless
　　folded hands.


And there came no morn,—no evening with its gentle
　　stars and moon,
But the sun amid the heavens made a broad unbroken
　　noon.

And anon far reaching westward, with its weight of
    burning air,
Lay an old and desolate ocean with a dead and glassy
    stare.


There my spirit wandered gazing, for the goal no time
    might reach,
With its weary feet unsandalled on the hard and heated
    beach.


This it is to feel uncared for, like a useless wayside
    stone,
This it is to walk in spirit through the desolate world
    alone!


Still I leaned across the marble, and a hand was on my
    arm,
And my soul came back unto me as 'twere summoned by
    a charm :


While a voice in gentlest whisper, breathed my name
    into my ear,
" Ah, Andrea, why this silence, why this shadow and
    this tear?"

Then I felt that I had wronged her, though I knew it
     not before;
I had feared that she would scorn me if I told the love
     I bore.

I had seen her, spoken to her, only twice or thrice per-
     chance;
And her mien was fine and stately, and all heaven was in
     her glance.

She had praised my humble labours, the conception and
     the art,—
She had said a thing of beauty nestled ever to her
     heart.

And I thought one pleasant morning when our eyes
     together met,
That her orbs in dewy splendour dropt beneath their
     fringe of jet.

Though her form and air were noble, yet a simple dress
     she wore,
Like yon maiden by the cypress, which the vines are
     weeping o'er.

And she came all unattended,—her protection in her
    mien ;
And with somewhat of reluctance bade me call her name
    Christine.


Then that name became a music, and my dreams went to
    the time,
And my brain all day made verses, and her beauty filled
    the rhyme.


Never dreamed I that she loved me, but I felt it now the
    more ;
For her hand was laid upon me, and her eyes were
    brimming o'er.


Oh, she looked into my spirit, as the stars look in the
    stream,
Or as azure eyes of angels calm the trouble of a
    dream.


Then I told my love unto her, and her sighs came deep
    and long—
So yon peasant plays the measure, while the other leads
    the song.

Then with tender words we parted, only as true lovers
    can;
I for that deep love she bore me was a braver, better
    man.


I had lived unloved of any, only loving Art before;
Now I thought all things did love me, and I loved all
    things the more.


I had lived accursed of Fortune, lived in penury worse
    than pain;
But, when all the heaven was blackest, down it showered
    in golden rain.


I was summoned to the palace, to the presence of the
    Duke,
Feeling hopes arise within me that no grandeur could
    rebuke.


Down he kindly came to meet me, but I thought the
    golden thróne
Upon which my love had raised me, was not lower than
    his own.

Then he grasped my hand with fervour, and I gave as
    warm return,
For I felt a noble nature in my very fingers burn.


And I would not bow below him, if I could not rise
    above,
For I felt within my bosom all the majesty of Love.


" Sir," said he, " your fame has reached me, and I fain
    would test your skill—
Carve me something, Signior; follow the free fancy of
    your will.


Carve me something—an Apollo, or a Dian with her
    hounds;
Or Adonis, dying, watching the young life flow from his
    wounds;—


Or a dreamy-lidded Psyché, with her Cupid on her
    knee;
Or a flying fretted Daphne, taking refuge in the tree.

But I will not dictate, Signior; I can trust your taste
    and skill—
In the ancient armoured chamber you may carve me what
    you will."


Then I thanked him as he left me—and I walked the
    armoured hall—
Even I, so late neglected, walked within the palace
    wall.


There were many suits of armour, some with battered
    breasts and casques;
And I thought the ancestral phantoms smiled upon me
    from their masks.


And my footsteps were elastic with an energy divine—
Never in those breasts of iron beat a heart as proud as
    mine !


There for days I walked the chamber with a spirit all
    inflamed,
And I thought on all the subjects which the generous
    Duke had named—

Thought of those, and thought of others, slowly thought
    them o'er and o'er,
Till my stormy brain went throbbing like the surf along
    the shore.


In despair I left the palace, sought my humble room
    again,
And my gentle Christine met me, and she smiled away
    my pain.


" Courage !" said she, and my courage leapt within me
    as she spake,
And my soul was sworn to trial and to triumph for her
    sake.


Who shall say that love is idle, or a weight upon the
    mind?
Friend ! the soul that dares to scorn it, hath in idle dust
    reclined.


I returned, and in the chamber piled the shapeless
    Adam-earth;
Piled it carelessly, not knowing to what form it might
    give birth.

There I leaned, and dreamed, above it, till the day went
  down the west,
And the darkness came unto me like an old familiar
  guest.


But I started, for a rustle swept athwart the solemn
  gloom !
And with light, like morn's horizon, gleamed the far end
  of the room !


Then a heavy sea of curtain, in a tempest rolled
  away !
Blessed Virgin ! how I trembled ! but it was not with
  dismay.


And my eyes grew large and larger, as I looked with
  lips apart ;
And my senses drank in beauty, till it drowned my
  happy heart.


There it stood, a living statue ! with its loosened locks
  of brown—
In an attitude angelic, with the folded hands dropt
  down.

But I could not see the features, for a veil was hanging
     there,
Yet so thin, that o'er the forehead I could trace the
     shadowy hair.


Then the veil became a trouble, and I wished that it
     were gone,
And I spake, 't was but a whisper, " Let thy features on
     me dawn !"


And the heavy sea of drapery stormed again across my
     sight,
Leaving me appalled with wonder, breathless in the
     sudden night.


But for days, where'er I turned me, still that blessed
     form was there,
As one looketh to the sunlight, then beholds it every-
     where.


And for days and days I laboured, with a soul in courage
     mailed;
And I wrought the nameless statue; but, alas! the face
     was veiled.

I had tried all forms of feature—every face of classic
    art—
Still the veil was there—I felt it—in my brain, and in
    my heart!


Sorrowing, I left the palace, and again I met Christine,
And she trembled as I told her of the vision I had
    seen.


And she sighed, "Ah, dear Andrea," while she clung
    unto my breast,
"What if this should prove a phantom, something fearful
    and unblest—


Something which shall pass between us?" and she
    clasped me with her arm;
"Nay," I answered, "love, I'll test it with a most
    angelic charm.


Let me gaze upon thy features, love, and fear not for
    the rest;
They shall exorcise the spirit if it be a thing unblest!"

Then I hurried to the statue, where so often I had
    failed,
And I made the face of Christine, and it stood no longer
    veiled !


With a flush upon my forehead, then I called the Duke—
    he came,
And in rustling silks beside him walked his tall and
    stately dame ;


And they looked upon the statue—then on me with
    stern surprise ;
Then they looked upon each other with a wonder in their
    eyes !


" What is this ?" spake out the Duchess, with her gaze
    fixed on the Duke ;
" What is this ?" and me he questioned in a tone of sharp
    rebuke.


Like a miserable echo, I the question asked again—
And he said, " It is our daughter ! your presumption for
    your pain !"

But asudden from the curtain, in her jewelled dress
    complete,
Swept a maiden in her beauty, and she dropped before
    his feet—


And she cried, "O! father—mother, cast aside that
    frowning mien;
And forgive my own Andrea, and forgive your child
    Christine!


O! forgive us: for, believe me, all the fault was mine
    alone!"
And they granted her petition, and they blessed us as
    their own.

# THE FAIRER LAND.


ALL the night, in broken slumber,
  I went down the world of dreams,
Through a land of war and turmoil
  Swept by loud and labouring streams,
Where the masters wandered, chanting
  Ponderous and tumultuous themes.


Chanting from unwieldy volumes
  Iron maxims stern and stark,
Truths that swept, and burst, and stumbled
  Through the ancient rifted dark;
Till my soul was tossed and worried,
  Like a tempest-driven bark.

But anon, within the distance,
　　Stood the village vanes aflame,
And the sunshine, filled with music,
　　To my oriel casement came;
While the birds sang pleasant valentines
　　Against my window frame.


Then by sights and sounds invited,
　　I went down to meet the morn,
Saw the trailing mists roll inland
　　Over rustling fields of corn,
And from quiet hillside hamlets
　　Heard the distant rustic horn.


There, through daisied dales and byways,
　　Met I forms of fairer mould,
Pouring songs for very pleasure—
　　Songs their hearts could not withhold—
Setting all the birds a-singing
　　With their delicate harps of gold.


Some went plucking little lily-bells,
　　That withered in the hand;

Some, where smiled a summer ocean,
  Gathered pebbles from the sand;
Some, with prophet eyes uplifted,
  Walked unconscious of the land.

Through that Fairer World I wandered
  Slowly, listening oft and long,
And as one behind the reapers,
  Without any thought of wrong,
Loitered, gleaning for my garner
  Flowery sheaves of sweetest song.
6

# ARISE.

I.

THE shadow of the midnight hours
　　Falls like a mantle round my form;
And all the stars, like autumn flowers,
　　Are banished by the whirling storm.
The demon-clouds throughout the sky
　　Are dancing in their strange delight,
While winds unwearied play;—but I
　　Am weary of the night.
Then rise, sweet maiden mine, arise,
And dawn upon me with thine eyes.

## II.

The linden, like a lover, stands
   And taps against thy window pane;—
The willow with its slender hands
   Is harping on the silver rain.
I've watched thy gleaming taper die,
   And hope departed with the light—
The winds unwearied play;—but I
   Am weary of the night.
Then rise, sweet maiden mine, arise,
And dawn upon me with thine eyes.


## III.

The gentle morning comes apace,
   And smiling bids the night depart;
Rise, maiden, with thy orient face,
   And smile the shadow from my heart!
The clouds of night affrighted fly—
   Yet darkness seals my longing sight—
All nature gladly sings—while I
   Am weary of the night.
Then rise, sweet maiden mine, arise,
And dawn upon me with thine eyes.

# THE MAID OF LINDEN LANE.

Little maiden, you may laugh
That you see me wear a staff,
But your laughter is the chaff
   From the melancholy grain.
Through the shadows long and cool
You are tripping down to school;
But your teacher's cloudy rule
Only dulls the shining pool
   With its loud and stormy rain.


There's a higher lore to learn
Than his knowledge can discern,
There's a valley deep and dern
   In a desolate domain;

But for this he has no chart—
Shallow science, shallow art!
Thither—oh, be still, my heart—
One too many did depart
  From the halls of Linden Lane.


I can teach you better things;
For I know the secret springs
Where the spirit wells and sings
  Till it overflows the brain.
Come, when eve is closing in,
When the spiders gray begin,
Like philosophers, to spin
Misty tissues, vain and thin,
  Through the shades of Linden Lane.


While you sit as in a trance,
Where the moon-made shadows dance,
From the distaff of Romance
  I will spin a silken skein:
Down the misty years gone by
I will turn your azure eye;
You shall see the changeful sky
Falling dark or hanging high
  Over the halls of Linden Lane.

Come, and sitting by the trees,
Over long and level leas,
Stretched between us and the seas,
　　I can point the battle-plain :
If the air comes from the shore
We may hear the billows roar;
But oh ! never, never more
Shall the wind come as of yore
　　To the halls of Linden Lane.


Those were weary days of woe,
Ah ! yes, many years ago,
When a cruel foreign foe
　　Sent his fleets across the main.
Though all this is in your books,
There are countless words and looks,
Which, like flowers in hidden nooks,
Or the melody of brooks,
　　There's no volume can retain.


Come, and if the night be fair,
And the moon be in the air,
I can tell you when and where
　　Walked a tender loving twain :

Though it cannot be, alas !
Yet, as in a magic glass,
We will sit and see them pass
Through the long and rustling grass
    At the foot of Linden Lane.

Yonder did they turn and go,
Through the level lawn below,
With a stately step and slow,
    And long shadows in their train :
Weaving dreams no thoughts could mar,
Down they wandered long and far,
Gazing toward the horizon's bar,
On their love's appointed star
    Rising in the Lion's Mane.

As across a summer sea,
Love sailed o'er the quiet lea,
Light as only love may be,
    Freighted with no care or pain.
Such the night; but with the morn
Brayed the distant bugle-horn—
Louder ! louder ! it was borne—
Then were anxious faces worn
    In the halls of Linden Lane.

With the trumpet's nearer bray,
Flashing but a league away,
Saw we arms and banners gay
 Stretching far along the plain.
Neighing answer to the call,
Burst our chargers from the stall;
Mounted, here they leaped the wall,
There the stream : while in the hall
 Eyes were dashed with sudden rain.


Belted for the fiercest fight,
And with swimming plume of white,
Passed the lover out of sight
 With the hurrying hosts amain.
Then the thunders of the gun
On the shuddering breezes run,
And the clouds o'erswept the sun,
Till the heavens hung dark and dun
 Over the halls of Linden Lane.


Few that joined the fiery fray
Lived to tell how went the day;
But that few could proudly say
 How the foe had fled the plain.

Long the maiden's eyes did yearn
For her cavalier's return;
But she watched alone to learn
That the valley deep and dern
  Was her desolate domain.


Leave your books awhile apart;
For they cannot teach the heart;
Come, and I will show the chart
  Which shall make the mystery plain
I can tell you hidden things
Which your knowledge never brings;
For I know the secret springs
Where the spirit wells and sings,
  Till it overflows the brain.


Ah, yes, lightly sing and laugh—
Half a child and woman half;
But your laughter is the chaff
  From the melancholy grain;
And, ere many years shall fly,
Age will dim your laughing eye,
And like me you'll totter by;
For remember, love, that I
  Was the Maid of Linden Lane.

# THE SWISS STREET-SINGER.

THROW up the glassy casement wide,
And fling the heavy blinds aside,
To let the sunshine and the tide
Of music through the chamber glide.
Oh, list! it is a maiden young,
Who singeth in a foreign tongue;
She poureth songs in strangest guise,
In words translated by her eyes.
      Come, youth and childhood, form the ring,
      And, maidens, from the window lean,
      To bid the exile Switzer sing,
      And strike the trembling tambourine!

The glistening azure in her eye
Hath something of her native sky;
The music of the rill and breeze
Are mingled in her melodies;
And in her form's tall graceful lines
There's something of the mountain pines;
And, oh, believe her soul may glow
As purely as the Alpine snow.
   Come, youth and childhood, form the ring,
   And, maidens, from the window lean,
   To bid the exile Switzer sing,
   And strike the trembling tambourine!


Oh, gaze not on her scornfully,
For, gentle lady, like to thee,
That wandering maiden well may be
Acquaint with pain and misery,—
And sad remembrance prompts the lay
That telleth of the far away;
While wildly in her music swell
The glory, name, and land of Tell!
   Then, youth and childhood, form the ring,
   And, maidens, from the window lean,
   To bid the exile Switzer sing,
   And strike the trembling tambourine!

# A LEAF FROM THE PAST.

INSCRIBED TO HENRY W. LONGFELLOW.

WITH thee, dear friend, though far away,
I walk, as on some vanished day,
And all the past returns in beautiful array.


With thee I still pace to and fro
Along the airy portico,
And gaze upon the flowers and river winding slow,


And there, as in some fairy realm,
I hear the sweet birds overwhelm
The fainting air with music from the lofty elm.

And hear the winged winds, like bees,
Go swarming in the tufted trees,
Or dropping low away, o'erweighed with melodies.


We walk beneath the cedar's eaves,
Where statued Ceres, with her sheaves,
Stands sheltered in a bower of trailing vines and leaves.


Or strolling by the garden fence,
Drinking delight with every sense,
We watch th' encamping sun throw up his golden tents.


With thee I wander as of old,
When fall the linden's leaves of gold,
Or when old winter whitely mantles all the wold.


As when the low salt marsh was mown,
With thee I idly saunter down
Between the long white village and the towered town.


I see the sultry bridge and long,
The river where the barges throng—
The bridge and river made immortal in thy song.

In dreams like these, of calm delight,
I live again the wintry night,
When all was dark without, but all within was bright—


When she, fit bride for such as thou,
She with the quiet, queenly brow,
Read from the minstrel's page with tuneful voice and low.


Still in the crowd or quiet nook,
I hear thy tone—behold thy look—
Thou speakest with thine eyes as from a poet's book.


I listen to thy cheering word,
And sadness, like the affrighted bird,
Flies fast, and flies afar, until it is unheard.

# ROSALIE.

## A BALLAD.


Full many dreamy summer days,
 Full many wakeful summer nights,
Fair Rosalie had walked the ways
  Wherein young Love delights.


Love took her by the willing hand—
 And oft she kissed the smiling boy—
He led her through his native land,
  The innocent fields of Joy.

As oft the evening tryste was set,
In cedarn grottoes far apart,
That young and lovely maiden met
The Minstrel of her heart.


Then Time, like some celestial barque,
With viewless sails and noiseless oars,
Conveyed them through the starry dark
Beyond the midnight shores.


And once he sang enchanted words,
In music fashioned to her choice,
Until the many dreaming birds
Learned beauty from his voice.


He sang to her of charmèd realms,
Of streams and lakes discerned by chance,
Of fleets, with golden prows and helms,
Deep freighted with romance;


Of vales, of purple mountains far,
With flowers below and stars above,
And of all homelier things that are
Made beautiful by Love;

Of rural days, when harvest sheaves
　　Along the heated uplands glow,
Or when the forest mourns its leaves,
　　And nests are full of snow.


He sang how evil evermore
　　Keeps ambush near our holiest ground,
But how an angel guards the door
　　Wherever Love is found.


Even while he sang new flowers had bloomed,
　　New stars looked through the river mist,
And suddenly the moon illumed
　　The temple of their tryste.


And with those flowers he crowned her there,
　　With vows which Time should not revoke;
Then from the nearest bough his hair
　　She bound with druid oak.


Oh, moon and stars, oh, leaves and flowers,
　　Ye heard their plighted accents then—
And heard within those sacred bowers
　　The tramp of armèd men!

7

Her father spake; his angry word
    The youth returned in keener heat;
But when replied the old man's sword,
    The youth lay at his feet.


And as a dreamer breathless, weak,
    From some immeasured turret thrown,
For very terror cannot shriek,
    Fair Rosalie dropt down.


They raised her in her drowning swoon,
    And placed her on a palfrey white;
A statue, paler than the moon,
    They bore her through the night.


Loud rang the many horses' hoofs,
    Like forging hammers, fast and full;
To her they seemed to tread on woofs
    Of deep and noiseless wool.


And like a fated bridal flower,
    From some betrothèd bosom blown,
They bore her to her prison tower,
    And left her there alone.

And when the cool auroral air
    Had won her tangled dreams apart,
She found the blossoms in her hair—
      Their memory in her heart.


She rose and paced the chamber dim,
    And watched the dying moon and stars,
Until the sun's broad burning rim
      Blazed through the lattice bars.


About her face the warm light stole,
    And yet her eyes no radiance won;
For through the prison of her soul
      There streamed no morning sun.


The day went by; and o'er the vale
    She saw the rising river mist;
And like a bride subdued and pale,
      Arrayed her for the tryste,


In nuptial robes, long wrought by stealth,
    With opals looped, pearl-broidered hems:
And at her waist a cinctured wealth
      Of rare ancestral gems.

The stars came out, and by degrees
    She heard a distant music swell,
While through the intervening trees
    Sang the glad chapel bell.


She heard her name, and knew the call:
    At once the noiseless door swung wide;
She passed the shadowy stair and hall—
    And One was at her side.


One, whose dear voice had charmed her long,
    And wooed her spirit to delight,
With airs of wild unwritten song,
    On many a summer night.


They passed the village hand-in-hand!
    They gazed upon the minster towers,
And heard behind a singing band
    Of maidens bearing flowers.


Age blessed them as they gayly passed,
    And rosy children danced before,
Until with trembling hearts at last
    They gained the chapel door.

But music in its triumph brings
  New courage unto old and young;
And with a rustle, as of wings,
    The choir arose and sung.


And while the anthem, loud or low,
  Swung round them like a golden cloud,
They walked the aisle, subdued and slow,
    And at the altar bowed.


And sacred hands were o'er them spread,
  And blessings passed away in prayer;
And then the soul of music sped
    Once more throughout the air.


It swelled and dropped and waned and rose,
  With flights for ever skyward given,
Like birds whose pinions spread and close,
    And rise thereby to heaven.


A murmur, like the soft desire
  Of leafy airs, went up the skies,
And Rosalie beheld the choir
    On angel wings arise.

Bright angels all encompassed her,
　　An angel in the altar stood,
And all her train of maidens were
　　A wingèd multitude.


The chapel walls dissolved and swept
　　Away, like mists when winds arise,
For Rosalie that hour had kept
　　Her tryste in Paradise.

# THE STRANGER ON THE SILL.

Between broad fields of wheat and corn
Is the lowly home where I was born;
The peach-tree leans against the wall,
And the woodbine wanders over all;
There is the shaded doorway still,
But a stranger's foot has crossed the sill.

There is the barn—and, as of yore,
I can smell the hay from the open door,
And see the busy swallow's throng,
And hear the peewee's mournful song;
But the stranger comes—oh! painful proof—
His sheaves are piled to the heated roof.

There is the orchard—the very trees
Where my childhood knew long hours of ease,

And watched the shadowy moments run
Till my life imbibed more shade than sun:
The swing from the bough still sweeps the air,
But the stranger's children are swinging there.

There bubbles the shady spring below,
With its bulrush brook where the hazels grow;
'Twas there I found the calamus root,
And watched the minnows poise and shoot,
And heard the robin lave his wing:—
But the stranger's bucket is at the spring.

Oh, ye who daily cross the sill,
Step lightly, for I love it still;
And when you crowd the old barn eaves,
Then think what countless harvest sheaves
Have passed within that scented door
To gladden eyes that are no more.

Deal kindly with these orchard trees;
And when your children crowd your knees,
Their sweetest fruit they shall impart,
As if old memories stirred their heart:
To youthful sport still leave the swing,
And in sweet reverence hold the spring.

# ENDYMION.

WHAT time the stars first flocked into the blue
    Behind young Hesper, shepherd of the eve,
Sleep bathed the fair boy's lids with charmèd dew,
    Mid flowers that all day blossomed to receive
        Endymion.


Lo! where he lay encircled in his dream;
    The moss was glad to pillow his soft hair,
And toward him leaned the lily from the stream,
    The hanging vine waved wooing in the air
        Endymion.


The brook that erewhile won its easy way,
    O'errun with meadow grasses long and cool,
Now reeled into a fuller tide and lay
    Caressing in its clear enamoured pool
        Endymion.

And all the sweet, delicious airs that fan
    Enchanted gardens in their hour of bloom,
Blown through the soft invisible pipes of Pan,
    Breathed, 'mid their mingled music and perfume,
        Endymion.


The silvery leaves that rustled in the light,
    Sent their winged shadows o'er his cheek entranced;
The constellations wandered down the night,
    And whispered to the dew-drops where they danced,
        Endymion.


Lo! there he slept, and all his flock at will
    Went star-like down the meadow's azure mist;—
What wonder that pale Dian with a thrill
    Breathed on his lips her sudden love, and kissed
        Endymion!

# HAZEL DELL.

From the early bells of morning,
  Till the evening chimes resound,
In the busy world of labour,
  For my daily bread I'm bound,
With no hopes of more possessions
  Than six scanty feet of ground!

But my soul hath found an empire,
  Hid between two sister hills,
Where she dreams or roams at pleasure,
  Finding whatsoe'er she wills;
There sweet Hope her fairest promise
  With a lavish hand fulfils.

And the path that windeth thither,
  There's no mortal foot may tread,
For it leads to charmèd valleys,
  With enchanted blossoms spread,
Under groves of flowering poplars,
  Through the violets' purple bed.

Overveiled with vines and water,
  Dropt from many a hidden well,
Are the rocks which make the gateway;—
  And the water's silver bell,
Keeps the warder, Silence, wakeful
  At the gate of Hazel Dell!

Nor may any pass the warder
  Till the watchword they repeat;
They must go arrayed like angels,
  In their purity complete;
And the stave-supported pilgrim
  Lay the sandals from his feet!

And within the purple valley,
  Where perpetual summer teems,
Whisper silken-tonguèd runnels,
  Melting into larger streams,

Winding round through sun and shadow,
  Like a gentle maiden's dreams.


Then let labour hold me vassal,
  Since my soul can scorn his reign!
Even fetters for the body
  Were but bands of sand, and vain,
While the spirit thus can wander,
  Singing through its own domain!


In the long still hours of darkness,
  Stretched from weary chime to chime;
Thus beside my own Castalie
  I can gather flowers of rhyme,
And with all their fresh dew freighted,
  Fling them on the stream of time!

# A GLIMPSE OF LOVE.

She came as comes the summer wind,
  A gust of beauty to my heart;
Then swept away, but left behind
  Emotions which shall not depart.


Unheralded she came and went,
  Like music in the silent night;
Which, when the burthened air is spent,
  Bequeaths to memory its delight;

Or, like the sudden April bow
   That spans the violet-waking rain :
She bade those blessed flowers to grow
   Which may not fall or fade again.


Far sweeter than all things most sweet,
   And fairer than all things most fair,
She came and passed with footsteps fleet,
   A shining wonder in the air.

# LINES TO A BLIND GIRL.

BLIND as the song of birds,
  Feeling its way into the heart,—
Or as a thought ere it hath words,—
  As blind thou art :—

Or as a little stream
  A dainty hand might guide apart,
Or Love—young Love's delicious dream,—
  As blind thou art :—

Or as a slender bark,
  Where summer's varying breezes start—
Or blossoms blowing in the dark,—
  As blind thou art :—

Or as the Hope, Desire
  Leads from the bosom's crowded mart,
Deluded Hope, that soon must tire,—
  As blind thou art :—


The chrysalis that folds
  The wings that shall in light depart,
Is not more blind than that which holds
  The wings within thy heart.


For when thy soul was given
  Unto the earth, a beauteous trust,
To guard its matchless glory, Heaven
  Endungeoned it in dust.

8

# ONCE MORE INTO THE OPEN AIR.

Once more into the open air,
  Once more beneath the summer skies,
To fields and woods and waters fair,
  I come for all which toil denies.

I loiter down through sun and shade,
  And where the waving pastures bloom,
And near the mowers' swinging blade
  Inhale the clover's sweet perfume.

The brook which late hath drank its fill,
  Out-sings the merry birds above;
The river past the neighbouring hill
  Flows like a quiet dream of love.


Yon rider in the harvest plain,
  The master of these woods and fields,
Knows not how largely his domain
  To me its richest fulness yields.


He garners what he reaps and mows,
  But there is that he cannot take,
The love which Nature's smile bestows,
  The peace which she alone can make.

# LOVE'S GALLERY.

## PICTURE FIRST.

### MIRIAM.

FAIR Miriam's was an ancient manse
Upon the open plain:
It looked to ocean's dim expanse,
Saw miles of meadow pasture dance
Beside the breezy main.


A porch, with woodbines overgrown,
Faced eastward to the shore;
While Autumn's sun, through foliage brown,
'Twixt leaf and lattice flickered down
To tesselate the floor.

There walked fair Miriam;—as she stept
        A rustle thrilled the air;
Rare, starry gems her tresses kept,
While o'er her brow a crescent swept
        The darkness of her hair.


But she too oft had paced the hall
        To ponder chronicles which Time
Had given at many an interval—
Ancestral shadows on the wall
        Looking their pride sublime.


And she too well had learned their look,
        And wore upon her tender age
A haughtiness I could not brook—
I said, it is a glorious book,
        But dared not trust the page.


## PICTURE SECOND.

### BERTHA.

Mild Bertha's was a home withdrawn
        Beyond the city's din;

Tall Lombard trees hemmed all the lawn,
And up the long straight walks, a dawn
    Of blossoms shone within.


Along the pebble paths the maid
    Walked with the early hours,
With careful hands the vines arrayed,
And plucked the small intruding blade
    From formal plots of flowers.


A statued Dian to the air
    Bequeathed its mellow light;
She called the flying figure fair,
The forward eyes and backward hair,
    And praised the marble's white.


Her pulses coursed their quiet ways,
    From heart to brain controlled;
She read and praised in studied phrase
The bards whom it were sin to praise
    In measured words and cold.


I love the broad bright world of snow,
    And every strange device

Which makes the woods a frozen show,
The rivers hard and still—but, oh,
    Ne'er loved a heart of ice.


## PICTURE THIRD.

### MELANIE.

Within a dusky grove, where wound
    Great centenarian vines,
Binding the shadows to the ground,
The dark-eyed Melanie was found
    Walking between the pines.


A sudden night of hair was thrown
    About her shining neck;
All woes she buried in her own—
Her sea of sadness carried down
    All lighter thoughts to wreck.


The past was hers; the coming years
    No golden promise brought :—
She gazed upon the midnight spheres
To read her future; and the tears
    Sprang vassals to her thought.

She heard all night through her domain
　　　The river moan below;
The whip-poor-will and owlet's strain
Filled up the measure of her pain
　　　In streams of fancied woe.

Thus as the mournful Melanie
　　　Swept through my waking dream,
I said: Oh soul, still wander free,
It is not written thou shalt see
　　　Thy image in this stream.

## PICTURE FOURTII.

### AURELIA.

Where flamed a field of flowers—and where
　　　Sang noisy birds and brooks—
Aurelia to the frolic air
Shook down her wanton waves of hair,
　　　With laughter-loving looks.

Her large and lustrous eyes of blue,
　　　Dashed with the dew of mirth,
Bequeathed to all their brilliant hue;
She saw no shades, nor even knew
　　　She walked the heavy earth.

Her ringing laughter woke the dells
    When fell the autumn blight;—
She sang through all the rainy spells—
For her the snow was full of bells
    Of music and delight.


She swept on her bewildering way,
    By every pleasure kiss'd,—
Making a mirth of night and day;
A brook all sparkle and all spray,
    Dancing itself to mist.


I love all bright and happy things,
    And joys which are not brief;
All sights and sounds whence pleasure springs;
But weary of the harp whose strings
    Are never tuned to grief.


## PICTURE FIFTH.

### AMY.

Round Amy's home were pleasant trees—
    A quiet summer space

Of garden flowers and toiling bees;
Below the yellow harvest leas
   Waved welcome to the place.

And Amy she was very fair,
   With eyes nor dark nor blue;
And in her wavy chestnut hair
Were braided blossoms, wild and rare,
   Still shimmering with the dew.

Her pride was the unconscious guise
   Which to the pure is given:
Her gentle prudence broke to sighs,
And smiles were native to her eyes,
   As are the stars to heaven.

Here love, said I, thy rest shall be,
   Oh, weary, world-worn soul!
Long tossed upon this shifting sea,
Behold, at last the shore for thee
   Displays the shining goal.

Dear Amy, lean above me now,
   And smooth aside my hair,
And bless me with thy tender vow,
And kiss all memories from my brow,
   Till thou alone art there.

# THE MINERS.

Burrow, burrow, like the mole,
Ye who shape the columned caves!
Ye are black with clinging coal,
Black as fiery Afric's slaves!
Sink the shadowy shaft afar
Deep into our native star!
Rend her iron ribs apart,
Where her hidden treasures are,
Nestled near her burning heart!
Dig, nor think how forests grow
Above your heads—how waters flow
Responsive to the song of birds—
How blossoms paint in silent words
What hearts may feel but cannot know!

Dig ye, where no day is seen;
Vassals in the train of Night,
Build the chambers for your Queen,
Where with starless locks she lies,
Robbed of all her bright disguise!
There no precious dews alight,
None but what the cavern weeps,
Down its scarred and dusky face!
There's no bird in all the place;
Not a simple flower ye mark,
Not a shrub or vine that creeps
Through the long, long Lapland dark!
Burrow, burrow, like the mole,
Dark of face, but bright of soul!
Labour is not mean or low!
Ye achieve, with every blow,
Something higher than ye know!
Though your sight may not extend
Through your labours to the end,
Every honest stroke ye give,
Every peril that ye brave
In the dark and dangerous cave,
In some future good shall live!

# THE WINNOWER.

Sings a maiden by a river,
   Sings and sighs alternately;
In my heart shall flow for ever,
   Like a stream, her melody.
In her hair of flaxen hue
   Tend'rest buds and blossoms gleam;
And her beauty glows as through
   Hazy splendours of a dream.
Like her melody's rich bars—
Or a golden flood of stars,—
Rustling like a summer rain,
Through her fingers falls the grain,

Swells her voice in such sweet measure,
I must join for very pleasure;
But my lay shall be of her,
Bright and lovely Winnower!

When her song to laughter merges,
  Melts the music of her tongue,
Like a streamlet's silver surges
  Over golden pebbles flung.
From her hands the grainless chaff
  On the light wind dances free;
But a sigh will check her laugh,—
  "So much worthlessness, ah me,
Mingles with the good!" saith she.
Yet the grain is fair to see.
Laughter, like some sweet surprise,
Lights again her dewy eyes,
And her song hath drowned her sighs;
Therefore will I sing of her,
Bright and lovely Winnower!

Down beside as fair a river
  Sings the Maiden Poesy,
In my heart shall flow for ever
  Her undying melody.

Through her rosy fingers fall
   Golden grains of richest thought ;
While the grainless chaff is all
   By the scattering breezes caught :—
   So much worthlessness, ah me,
   Mingles with the good !'' saith she.
Yet the grain is bright to see,
Therefore laughs she merrily !
Laughs and sings in such sweet measure,
I must join for very pleasure—
While my heart keeps time with her,
I will praise the Winnower !

# FRAGMENTS FROM THE REALM OF DREAMS.



OFT have I wandered through the Realm of Dreams,
By shadowy mountains and clear running streams,
Catching at times strange transitory gleams
Of Eden vistas, glimmering through a haze
Of floral splendour, where the birds, ablaze
With colour, streaked the air like flying stars,
With momentary bars ;
And heard low music breathe above, around,
As if the air within itself made sound,—
As if the soul of Melody were pent
Within some unseen instrument

Hung in a viewless tower of air,
And with enchanted pipes beguiled its own despair.
But stranger than all other dreams which led,
Asleep or waking, my adventurous tread,
Were these which came of late to me
Through fields of slumber, and did seem to be
Wrapped in an awful robe of prophecy.


I walked the woods of March, and through the boughs
The earliest bird was calling to his spouse;
And in the sheltered nooks
Lay spots of snow,
Or with a noiseless flow
Stole down into the brooks;
And where the springtime sun had longest shone
The violet looked up and found itself alone.
Anon I came unto a noisy river,
And felt the bridge beneath me sway and quiver;
Below, the hungry waters howled and hissed,
And upward blew a blinding cloud of mist;
But there the friendly Iris built its arch,
And I in safety took my onward march.
Now coming to a mighty hill,
Along the shelvy pathway of a rill

Which danced itself to foam and spray,
I clomb my steady way.
It may be that the music of the brook
Gave me new strength—It may be that I took
Fresh vigour from the mountain air
Which cooled my cheek and fanned my hair;
Or was it that adown the breeze
Came sounds of wondrous melodies,—
Strange sounds as of a maiden's voice
Making her mountain home rejoice?
Following that sweet strain, I mounted still
And gained the highest hemlocks of the hill,
Old guardians of a little lake, which sent
Adown the brook its crystal merriment,
Blessing the valley where the planter went
Sowing the furrowed mould and whistling his content.
Through underwood of laurel, and across
A little lawn shoe-deep with sweetest moss,
I passed, and found the lake, which, like a shield
Some giant long had ceased to wield,
Lay with its edges sunk in sand and stone,
With ancient roots and grasses overgrown;
But far more beautiful and rare
Than any strange device that e'er
Glittered upon the azure field
Of ancient warrior's polished shield,

Was the fair vision which did lie
Embossed upon the burnished lake,
And in its sweet repose did make
A second self that sang to the inverted sky.
Not she who lay on banks of Thornless flowers
Ere stole the serpent into Eden's bowers;
Not she who rose from Neptune's deep abodes,
The wonder of Olympian Gods;
Nor all the fabled nymphs of wood or stream
Which blest the Arcadian's dream,
Could with that floating form compare,
Lying with her golden harp and hair
Bright as a cloud in the sunset air.
Her tresses gleamed with many stars,
And on her forehead one, like Mars,
A lovely crown of light dispread
Around her shining head.
And now she touched her harp and sung
Strange songs in a forgotten tongue;
And as my spirit heard, it seemed
To feel what it had lived or dreamed
In other worlds beyond our skies,—
In ancient spheres of Paradise;
And as I gazed upon her face,
It seemed that I could dimly trace

Dear lineaments long lost of yore
Upon some unremembered shore,
Beyond an old and infinite sea,
In the realm of an unknown century.
For very joy I clapped my hands,
And leaped upon the nearer sands!—
A moment, and the maiden glanced
Upon me where I stood entranced;
Then noiselessly as moonshine falls
Adown the ocean's crystal walls,
And with no stir or wave attended,
Slowly through the lake descended;
Till from her hidden form below
The waters took a golden glow,
As if the star which made her forehead bright
Had burst and filled the lake with light!
Long standing there I watched in vain,—
The vision would not rise again.


Again, in sleep, I walked by singing streams,
And it was May-day in my Realm of Dreams :—
The flowering pastures and the trees
Were full of noisy birds and bees;
And swinging roses, like sweet censers, went,
The village children making merriment,

Followed by older people;—as they passed
One beckoned, and I joined the last.
We crossed the meadow, crossed the brook,
And through the scented woodland took
Our happy way, until we found
An open space of vernal ground;
And there around the flowery pole
I joined the joyous throng and sang with all my soul!
But when the little ones had crowned their queen,
And danced their mazes to the wooded scene
To hunt the honeysuckles, and carouse
Under the spice-wood boughs,—
I turned, and saw with wondering eye
A maiden in a bower near by
Wreathed with unknown blossoms, such as bloom
In orient isles with wonderful perfume.
And she was very beautiful and bright;
And in her face was much of that strange light
Which on the mountain lake had blessed my sight;
Her speech was like the echo of that song
Which on the hill-side made me strong.
Now with a wreath, now with a coin she played,
Pursuing a most marvellous trade—
Buying the lives of young and old,
Some with Fame, and some with gold!

And there with trembling steps I came,
But ere I asked for gold or fame,
Or ere I could announce my name
The wreath fell withered from her head,
And from her face the mask was shed;
Her mantle dropped—and lo! the morning sun
Looked on me through a nameless skeleton!
Again I stood within the Realm of Dreams,
At midnight, on a huge and shadowy tower;
And from the east the full moon shed her beams,
And from the sky a wild meteoric shower
Startled the darkness; and the night
Was full of ominous voices and strange light,
Like to a madman's brain;—below
Prophetic tongues proclaiming woe
Echoed the sullen roar
Of Ocean on the neighbouring shore;
And in the west a forest caught the sound,
And bore it to its utmost bound.
And then, for hours, all stood as to behold
Some great event by mighty seers foretold;
And all the while the moon above the sea
Grew strangely large and red,—and suddenly,
Followed by a myriad stars,
Swung at one sweep into the western sky,

And, widening with a melancholy roar,
Broke to a hundred flaming bars,
Grating the heavens as with a dungeon door.
Then to that burning gate
A radiant spirit came, and through the grate
Smiled till I knew the Angel, Fate!
And in its hand a golden key it bore
To open that celestial door.
Sure, I beheld that angel thrice;
Twice met on earth, it mocked me twice;
But now behind those bars it beamed
Such love as I had never dreamed,
Smiling my prisoned soul to peace
With eyes that promised quick release;
And looks thus spake to looks, where lips on earth were
  dumb,
      "Behold, behold the hour is come!"

# "COME, GENTLE TREMBLER."

Come, gentle trembler, come—for see,
  Our hearths have lost their native fires;
The vacant world invites us,—we
  Must go the heirless heirs of countless sires.


Let us away, the wild wolf's home
  Were not so desolate as ours;
Beside the singing brooks we'll roam,
  And seek a sweet community of flowers.


Here are the dwellings whence the few
  We loved, departed; where they lead
We follow—these their tombs;—but who
  Shall write our epitaphs, and who shall read?

Hark, how the light winds flow and ebb
    Along the open halls forlorn;
See how the spider's dusty web
    Floats at the casement, tenantless and torn!


The old, old Sea, as one in tears,
    Comes murmuring with its foamy lips,
And knocking at the vacant piers,
    Calls for its long-lost multitude of ships.


Against the stone-ribbed wharf, one hull
    Throbs to its ruin like a breaking heart:
Oh, come, my breast and brain are full
    Of sad response—Let Silence keep the mart!

# THE FROZEN GOBLET.

The night was dark, the winds were loud,
The storm hung low in a swinging cloud;
The blaze on my chamber lamp was dim,
And athwart my brain began to swim
Those visions that only swim and sweep
Under the wavering wings of sleep:—
And suddenly into my presence came
A Spectre, thin as that dismal flame
That burns and beams, a moving lamp,
Where the dreary fogs of night encamp.

Her lips were pale, her cheeks were white,
Her eyes were full of phantom light—
    Once, twice, thrice,
A goblet wrought to a rare device
She held to fevered lips of mine;
But mocked them with its frozen wine,
Till they were numb on the dusky ice.


I could not speak, I could not stir,
I could do nought but look at her;
Nought but look in her wonderful eyes,
And lose me in their mysteries.
The goblet shone, the goblet glowed,
But from its rim no liquid flowed.
Its sides were bright with pictures rare
Of demons foul and angels fair,
And Life and Death o'er Youth contending,
And Love on luminous wings descending,
Celestial cities with golden domes,
And caverns full of labouring gnomes.
    Once, twice, thrice,
That goblet wrought to a rare device
She held to fevered lips of mine,
But mocked them with its frozen wine,
Till they were numb on the dusky ice.

Loud rang the bell through the stormy air,
And the clock replied on the shadowy stair,
And Chanticleer awoke and flung
The echo from its silvery tongue.
All nature with a sudden noise
Proclaimed the momentary poise
Of that invisible beam, that weighs
At midnight the divided days.
The Phantom beckoned and turned away,
I had no power to speak or stay :—
We passed the dusky corridor,
Her sandal gems illumed the floor,
And with a ruddy, phosphor light,
The frozen goblet lit the night.
          Once, twice, thrice,
That goblet wrought to a rare device
She held to fevered lips of mine,
But mocked them with its frozen wine,
Till they were numb on the dusky ice.


She led me through enchanted woods,
Through deep and haunted solitudes,
By threatening cataracts, and the edges
Of high and dizzy mountain ledges,

And over bleak and perilous ridges,
To frail and air-suspended bridges,
Where, in the muffled dark beneath,
Invisible rivers talked of death,
Until, for very sympathy
With the unfathomed mystery,
I cried, " Here I resign my breath,
Here let me taste the cup of Death !"
      Once, twice, thrice,
That goblet wrought to a rare device
She held again to lips of mine,
But mocked them with its frozen wine,
Till they were numb on the dusky ice.

And then a voice within me said,
" Wouldst thou journey to the dead ?—
Shed this mantle, and pass for ever
Into the black, eternal river ?—
For very sympathy, depart
From the tumult of this heart ?
Know'st thou not that mightier river,
Rolling on in darkness ever,
Ever sweeping, coiling, boiling,
Howling, fretting, wailing, toiling,
Where every wave that breaks on shore
Is a human heart that can bear no more ?"

Once, twice, thrice,
That goblet wrought to a rare device
She held to fevered lips of mine,
But mocked them with the frozen wine,
Till they were numb on the dusky ice.

And then in sorrow and shame I cried,
" Oh, take me to that river's side,
And I will shun the languid shore,
And plunge me into the dark uproar,
And drink of the waters till they impart
A generous sense, and a human heart."
And all at once, around me rose
A mingled mutiny of woes,
And my soul discerned these sounds to be
The wail of a wide humanity;
Till my bosom heaved responsive sighs,
And tremulous tears were in my eyes.
Once, twice, thrice,
That goblet wrought to a rare device
She held to fevered lips of mine,
And at their instant touch, the wine
Flowed freely from the dusky ice.

I drank new life, I could not stop,
But drained it to its latest drop,

Till the Phantom with the goblet rare
Dissolved into the shadowy air—
Dissolved into the outer gloom,
And once more I was in my room;
Yet oft before my waking eyes
The figures of that goblet rise—
The angels and the fiends at strife,
And Youth 'twixt warring Death and Life—
The domes—the gnomes—mysterious things!
And Love descending on bright wings.

  Once, twice, thrice,
That goblet wrought to a rare device
Fair Memory holds to lips of mine,
And bathes them with the sacred wine,
The tribute of that dusky ice.

# THE CITY OF THE HEART.

THE heart is a city teeming with life—
Through all its gay avenues, rife
     With gladness
      And innocent madness,
   Bright beings are passing along,
Too fleeting and fair for the eye to behold,
   While something of Paradise sweetens their song,
They are gliding away with their wild gushing ditty,
     Out of the city,
  Out of the beautiful gates of gold !

Through gates that are ringing
While to and fro swinging,
Swinging and ringing ceaselessly,
Like delicate hands that are clapped in glee,
Beautiful hands of infancy!


The heart is a city—and gay are the feet
That dance along
To the joyous beat
Of the timbrel that giveth a pulse to song.
Bright creatures enwreathed
With flowers and mirth,
Fair maidens bequeathed
With the glory of earth
Sweep through the long street, and singing await,
A moment await at the wonderful gate;
Every second of time there comes to depart
Some form that no more shall revisit the heart!
They are gliding away and breathing farewell—
How swiftly they pass
Through the gates of brass,
Through gates that are ringing
While to and fro swinging.
And making deep sounds, like the half-stifled swell
Of the far-away ring of a gay marriage bell!
10

The heart is a city with splendour bedight,
Where tread martial armies arrayed for the fight,
　　Under banner-hung arches,
　　To war-kindling marches,
　　To the fife and the rattle
　Of drums, with gay colours unfurled,
　　On, eager for battle,
To smite their bright spears on the spears of the
　　　　world !
Through noontime, through midnight, list, and thou'lt
　　　　hear
The gates swing in front, then clang in the rear.
　　Like a bright river flowing,
　　The war host is going,
　　And like to that river,
　　Returning, ah never !
Through daylight and darkness low thunder is heard
　　From the city that flings
　　Her iron-wrought wings,
Flapping the air like the wings of a bird !


The heart is a city—how sadly and slow,
　To and fro,
Covered with rust, the solemn gates go !

With meek folded palms,
With heads bending lowly,
Strange beings pass slowly,
Through the dull avenues chanting their psalms;
Sighing and mourning, they follow the dead
Out of the gates that fall heavy as lead—
Passing, how sadly, with echoless tread,
The last one is fled!
No more to be opened, the gates softly close,
And shut in a stranger who loves the repose;
With no sigh for the past, with no countenance of pity,
He spreads his black flag o'er the desolate city!

# THE BEGGAR OF NAPLES.

THE music of the marriage bell
Woke all the morning air to pleasure,
And breasts there were that rose and fell
To the delightful measure.
Oh, well it were if they might hear alway
The music of their nuptial day
Flowing, as o'er enchanted lakes and streams
Out of the land of dreams—
Sweet sounds that melt but never cease,
Dropped from celestial bells of peace.
Oh, well it were if those rare bridal flowers
Had drunken deep of life's perpetual dews,

Had drunken of those charmed showers
For ever falling in ambrosial hues
Through the far loving skies,
Beyond the flaming walls of long-lost Paradise;
Or grown beside that fabled river
Where it is spring-time ever;
Where, when the aged pilgrim stooped and drank,
He rose again upon that primrose bank
In all the bloom of youth to bloom for ever.
Ah, well for Beauty's transient bowers
If they might bud and blow in life's autumnal hours:—
For she, who wore that bridal wreath
Was Naples' noblest child;
The fairest maid that e'er beguiled
An Abbot of a prayerful breath.
And he who rode beside her there
Was Fame and Fortune's richest heir;
One who had come from foreign realms afar
To dazzle like a new-discovered star.
Yet as they passed between the crowd
He looked not scornfully nor proud,
But to the beggars thronging every side
Scattered the golden coin in plenteous rain,
And smiled to see their joy insane.
And passing, thus addressed the bride:—

"The merry bells make music sweet,
But never to the beggar's ear
Fell music half so sweet and clear
As the chime of gold when it strikes the street;
It drives their hearts to swifter swinging,
And fills their brains with gladder ringing
Than ever bells will swing or ring,
Even though the sturdy sacristan
Should labour the very best he can
To chime for the wedding of a king.
Such sights to me will always bring
The story of a beggar, who
Perchance has ofttimes begged of you;
And here the tale may well be told,
To while away this idle gait
That keeps us from our happy fate:
For time is very lame and old
Whene'er the surly graybeard brings
A prayed-for pleasure on his wings;
But robbing us of a joy can flee
As fleet of foot as Mercury.

" Avoiding every wintry shade,
The lazzaroni crawled to sunny spots,—
At every corner miserable knots
Pursued their miserable trade;

And held the sunshine in their asking palms,
Which gave unthanked its glowing alms,
Thawing the blood until it ran
As wine within a vintage runs.
And there was one among that begging clan,
One of Italia's listless dreamy sons,
A native Neapolitan—
A boy whose cheeks had drawn their olive tan
From fifteen summer suns.
Long had he stood with naked feet
Upon the lava of the street,
With shadowy eyes cast down,
Making neither a smile nor frown,
And in the crowd he stood alone,
Alone with empty hanging hands,
And through his brain the idle dreams
Slid down like idle sands;
Or hung like mists o'er sleeping streams
In uninhabitable lands.
To him, I ween, the same,
All seasons went and came
Nor did ambition's pomp and show
Disturb his fancy's tranquil flow;
For, like the blossom of the soil,
Existence was his only toil.

"One morn (the bells had summoned all to mass)
He knelt before the old cathedral door—
At such a place the wealthier who pass
Will throw a pious pittance to the poor,
Who kneel with face demure,
With their mute eyes and hands saying their 'alas!'
Oh, beautiful it was to see him there,
Looking his wordless prayer,
With solemn head depressed,
And hands laid crosswise on his breast,—
Such figures saw Murillo in his dream,
The painter and the pride of Spain;
With such he made his living canvas gleam,
As canvas touched by man may never gleam again.


"Upon the beggar's heart the matin hymn
Fell faint and dim
As when upon some margin of the sea
The fisher breathes the briny air,
And hears the far waves' symphony,
But hears it unaware.
The music from the lofty aisle,
And all the splendour of the sacred pile,—
The pictures hung at intervals
Like windows, giving from the walls

Clear glimpses of the days agone,
From that blest hour when over Bethlehem shone
The shepherd's Star, until that darker time
When groaned the earth aloud with agony sublime:—
All were unheeded,
And came, but as his breath;
Or if there came a thought, that thought unheeded
Even in its birth met death.
The names of Raphael,—Angelo,—Lorraine,—
Da Vinci,—Roso,—Titian,—and the rest,
Are sounds to thrill the Italian's soul and brain
With all the impulse native to his breast;
And Dante,—Petrarch,—these are mighty names
The meanest tongue with a true pride proclaims;
And Ariosto's song a loved bequest;
And Tasso's sung by all—by all is loved and blest.
But what cared he, the sunburnt beggar-boy?
All these bequeathed no other joy
Than did the silent stars,
Or morn or evening with their golden bars.
Or the great azure arch of day,
Or his own bright, unrivalled bay,
Or old Vesuvius' deathless flames—
And these to him alone were empty sights and names.

"Few were there who did any alms bestow,
For few will hear accustomed sounds of woe;

Yet there was one among that few
Who but a moment stopped,
And in the beggar's hands the silver dropped,
And shed the benediction of her smile.
Such smile as hers might well renew
A heart to its lost light, and might beguile
The shadow of a mourner's hour;
Such smiles are like the blessed dew
By evening shed upon a wayside flower,
Sinking to the heart of hearts with a miraculous
   power.
The earliest primrose of the spring,
Which at the brook-side suddenly in sight
Gleams like a water sprite;
And the first herald bird on southern wing,
Chanting his wild, enthusiastic rhyme
About the summer time—
Wake in the soul an instant, deep delight!
But there are eyes whose first sweet look
Outshines the primrose by the brook;
And there are lips whose simplest words
Outrival even the spring-time birds.
Ah, well, I ween, the beggar felt their power,
And wore them in his heart from that bright hour.
She passed—a maiden very young and fair,
Of an illustrious house the pride and heir;

She passed—but ah, she left
The miserable boy bereft !—
Bereft of all that quiet which had lain
Like a low mist within his brain,—
The idle fogs of some rank weedy isle
Hanging on the breezeless atmosphere,
Over a miasmatic mere ;—
All this the beauty of her smile
Had blown into a storm that would not rest again.
At once upstarting from his knees,
He watched her as she went ;
The blood awakened from its slothful case,
Through all his frame a flaming flood was sent.
He stood as with a statue's fixed surprise,
Great wonder making marble in his eyes !
She, like a morn, had dawned upon his soul ;
And now he saw the marvellous whole
Of that mysterious land,
And felt a sense of awe as they who stand
For the first time upon an alien strand,—
Some sailor of a foreign sea,
Who, from the smooth waves swinging lazily,
Is thrown upon a shore
Where life is full of noise and strife for evermore
He stood awake ! and suddenly there burst

The music of the organ on his brain,
And into every sense athirst
Dispensed a welcome rain.
Now that his soul had passed from its eclipse,
All things at once became a glorious show;
Now could he see the sainted pictures glow;
And instantly unto his lips
Rolled fragments of old song—
Fragments which had been thrown
Into his heart unknown,
And buried there had lain in silence deep and long.

"He saw his fellows kneel where he had knelt
With tattered garb and supplicating air;
And for the first time in his life he felt
How mean was his attire, and that his feet were bare.
He sighed and bit his lips, and passed away;
And from that day,
His fellows idly as before,
Without a hope, without a care,
Stood clustered in the sunny air,
But there the beggar boy was seen no more.

"His childhood, like a dry and sandy bar,
Lay all behind him as he hurled

His soul's hot bark to sea, and wide unfurled
The straining sail upon a billowy world.
And now he joined the sacred fleet afar,
And 'mid tempestuous waves of war
Defied the Saracen and Death,
And won the warrior's laurel wreath,
And gave his beggar name to Fame's industrious breath

"Years came and went, and no one missed the boy,
Nor wept his long farewell;
They little guessed how much their joy
Was of his deeds to tell.
And when he knew his native town
Had learned to talk of his renown,
The youth a bearded man returned;
And more than for renown he yearned
To see that blessed smile again
Which erst made beauty in his brain,
And ever in the van of war
Had shown a most propitious star.
He came, and she of whom he long had dreamed
With hopes which nought could e'er destroy,
In brighter beauty on him beamed,
And blessed him with a deeper joy;
Even she, the noblest lady of the land,
Bestowed on him her virgin hand!

Ah, sure it was the fairest alms
That ever blessed a beggar's palms !

"To him the chime which filled the skies
Upon his nuptial morn,
When down the loving breezes borne,
Did seem to be by angels rung
From silver bells of Paradise,
In golden turrets hung.
And she, who woke the boy to man,
As little dreamed, I guess, as now,
My gentle lady, as dost thou,
How proud she was to wed that barefoot Neapolitan."

# THE BRICKMAKER.

I.

Let the blinded horse go round
Till the yellow clay be ground,
And no weary arms be folded
Till the mass to brick be moulded.

In no stately structures skilled,
What the temple we would build?
Now the massive kiln is risen—
Call it palace—call it prison;
View it well: from end to end
Narrow corridors extend,—

Long, and dark, and smothered aisles :—
Choke its earthly vaults with piles
    Of the resinous yellow pine ;
Now thrust in the fettered fire—
Hearken ! how he stamps with ire,
    Treading out the pitchy wine ;
Wrought anon to wilder spells
    Hear him shout his loud alarms ;
    See him thrust his glowing arms
Through the windows of his cells.

But his chains at last shall sever ;
Slavery lives not for ever ;
And the thickest prison wall
Into ruin yet must fall ;
Whatsoever falls away
Springeth up again, they say ;
Then, when this shall break asunder,
And the fire be freed from under,
Tell us what imperial thing
From the ruin shall upspring ?

There shall grow a stately building,
    Airy dome and columned walls ;
Mottoes writ in richest gilding
    Blazing through its pillared halls.

In those chambers, stern and dreaded,
   They, the mighty ones, shall stand;
There shall sit the hoary-headed
   Old defenders of the land.


There shall mighty words be spoken,
   Which shall thrill a wondering world;
Then shall ancient bonds be broken,
   And new banners be unfurled.


But anon those glorious uses
   In these chambers shall lie dead,
And the world's antique abuses,
   Hydra-headed, rise instead.


But this wrong not long shall linger—
   The old capitol must fall;
For, behold! the fiery finger
   Flames along the fated wall!


## II.

Let the blinded horse go round
'Till the yellow clay be ground,

And no weary arms be folded
Till the mass to brick be moulded—
Till the heavy walls be risen,
And the fire is in his prison:
But when break the walls asunder,
And the fire is freed from under,
Say again what stately thing
From the ruin shall upspring?


There shall grow a church whose steeple
　　To the heavens shall aspire;
And shall come the mighty people
　　To the music of the choir.


On the infant, robed in whiteness,
　　Shall baptismal waters fall,
While the child's angelic brightness
　　Sheds a halo over all.


There shall stand enwreathed in marriage
　　Forms that tremble—hearts that thrill—
To the door Death's sable carriage
　　Shall bring forms and hearts grown still!

Decked in garments richly glistening,
   Rustling wealth shall walk the aisle;
And the poor without stand listening,
   Praying in their hearts the while.


There the veteran shall come weekly
   With his cane, oppressed and poor,
'Mid the horses standing meekly,
   Gazing through the open door.


But these wrongs not long shall linger—
   The presumptuous pile must fall;
For, behold! the fiery finger
   Flames along the fated wall!


### III.


Let the blinded horse go round
Till the yellow clay be ground;
And no weary arms be folded
Till the mass to brick be moulded—
Say again what stately thing
From the ruin shall upspring?

Not the hall with columned chambers,
    Starred with words of liberty,
Where the freedom-canting members
    Feel no impulse of the free;


Not the pile where souls in error
    Hear the words, " Go, sin no more !"
But a dusky thing of terror,
    With its cells and grated door.


To its inmates each to-morrow
    Shall bring in no tide of joy.
Born in darkness and in sorrow
    There shall stand the fated boy.


With a grief too loud to smother,
    With a throbbing, burning head—
There shall groan some desperate mother,
    Nor deny the stolen bread !


There the veteran, a poor debtor,
    Marked with honourable scars,
Listening to some clanking fetter,
    Shall gaze idly through the bars :

Shall gaze idly, not demurring,
  Though with thick oppression bowed;
While the many, doubly erring,
  Shall walk honoured through the crowd.


Yet these wrongs not long shall linger—
  The benighted pile must fall;
For, behold! the fiery finger
  Flames along the fated wall!


IV.


Let the blinded horse go round
Till the yellow clay be ground;
And no weary arms be folded
Till the mass to brick be moulded—
Till the heavy walls be risen
And the fire is in his prison.
Capitol, and church, and jail,
Like our kiln at last shall fail;
Every shape of earth shall fade;
But the Heavenly Temple made
For the sorely tried and pure,
With its Builder shall endure!

# SONG FOR A SABBATH MORNING.

Arise, ye nations, with rejoicing rise,
And tell your gladness to the listening skies;
Come out forgetful of the week's turmoil,
From halls of mirth and iron gates of toil;
Come forth, come forth, and let your joy increase
Till one loud pæan hails the day of peace.
Sing, trembling age, ye youths and maidens sing;
Ring, ye sweet chimes, from every belfry ring;
Pour the grand anthem till it soars and swells,
And heaven seems full of great aerial bells!

Behold the Morn from orient chambers glide,
With shining footsteps, like a radiant bride ;
The gladdened brooks proclaim her on the hills,
And every grove with choral welcome thrills.
Rise, ye sweet maidens, strew her path with flowers,
With sacred lilies from your virgin bowers ;
Go, youths, and meet her with your olive boughs ;
Go, age, and greet her with your holiest vows ;—
See where she comes, her hands upon her breast,
The sainted Sabbath comes, and smiles the world to rest.

# THE NAMELESS.

Come fill, my merry friends, to-night,
　And let the winds unheeded blow,
And we will wake the deep delight
　Which true hearts only know.
And ere the passing wine be done,
　Come drink to those most fair and dear,
And I will pledge a cup to one
　Who shall be nameless here.


Come fill, nor let the flagon stand,
　Till pleasure's voice shall drown the wind,
Nor heed old Winter's stormy hand
　Which shakes the window-blind.
And down the midnight hour shall run
　The brightest moments of the year;
While I will fill, my friends, to one
　Who shall be nameless here.

Pledge you to lips that smile in sleep,
    Whose dreams have strewed your path with flowers,
And to those sacred eyes that weep
    Whene'er your fortune lowers;
And charm the night, ere it be done,
    With names that are for ever dear,
While I must pour and quaff to one
    Who shall be nameless here.

To her I proudly poured the first
    Inspiring beaker of the Rhine,
And still it floods my veins as erst
    It filled the German vine.
And when her memory, like the sun,
    Shall widen down my dying year,
My latest cup will be to one
    Who shall be nameless here.

# INDIAN SUMMER.

It is the season when the light of dreams
  Around the year in golden glory lies;—
  The heavens are full of floating mysteries,
And down the lake the veilèd splendour beams!
  Like hidden poets lie the hazy streams,
Mantled with mysteries of their own romance,
While scarce a breath disturbs their drowsy trance.
  The yellow leaf which down the soft air gleams,
Glides, wavers, falls, and skims the unruffled lake.
  Here the frail maples and the faithful firs
By twisted vines are wed.  The russet brake
  Skirts the low pool; and starred with open burrs
  The chestnut stands—But when the north-wind stirs,
How, like an armèd host, the summoned scene shall wake!

# A MORNING, BUT NO SUN.

The morning comes, but brings no sun;
The sky with storm is overrun;
And here I sit in my room alone,
And feel, as I hear the tempest moan,
Like one who hath lost the last and best,
The dearest dweller from his breast!
For every pleasant sight and sound,
The sorrows of the sky have drowned;
bell within the neighbouring tower,
blurred and distant through the shower;

Look where I will, hear what I may,
All, all the world seems far away !
The dreary shutters creak and swing,
The windy willows sway and fling
A double portion of the rain
Over the weeping window pane.
But I, with gusty sorrow swayed,
Sit hidden here, like one afraid,
And would not on another throw
One drop of all this weight of woe !

# TO THE MASTER BARDS.

Ye mighty masters of the song sublime,
Who, phantom-like, with large unwavering eyes,
Stalk down the solemn wilderness of Time,
Reading the mysteries of the future skies;
Oh, scorn not earth because it is not heaven;
Nor shake the dust against us from your feet,
Because we have rejected what was given!
Still let your tongues the wondrous theme repeat!
Though ye be friendless in this solitude,
Quick-wingèd thoughts, from many an unborn year,
God-sent, shall feed ye with prophetic food,
Like those blest birds which fed the ancient Seër!
And Inspiration, like a wheelèd flame,
Shall bear ye upward to eternal fame!

# "OH, WHEREFORE SIGH?"

Oh, wherefore sigh for what is gone,
  Or deem the future all a night?
From darkness through the rosy dawn
  The stars go singing into light.

And to the pilgrim lone and gray,
  One thought shall come to cheer his breast;—
The evening sun but fades away
  To find new morning in the west.

# THE WAY.

A WEARY, wandering soul am I,
  O'erburthened with an earthly weight;
A pilgrim through the world and sky,
  Toward the Celestial Gate.

Tell me, ye sweet and sinless flowers,
  Who all night gaze upon the skies,
Have ye not in the silent hours
  Seen aught of Paradise?

Ye birds, that soar and sing, elate
  With joy, that makes your voices strong,
Have ye not at the golden gate
  Caught somewhat of your song?


Ye waters, sparkling in the morn,
  Ye seas, which glass the starry night,
Have ye not from the imperial bourn
  Caught glimpses of its light?


Ye hermit oaks, and sentinel pines,
  Ye mountain forests, old and gray,
In all your long and winding lines,
  Have ye not seen the way?


O! moon, among thy starry bowers,
  Know'st thou the path the angels tread?
Seest thou beyond thy azure towers
  The shining gates dispread?


Ye holy spheres, that sang with earth,
  When earth was still a sinless star,
Have the immortals heavenly birth
  Within your realms afar?

And thou, O sun! whose light unfurls
    Bright banners through unnumbered skies,
Seest thou among thy subject worlds
    The radiant portals rise?


All, all are mute! and still am I
    O'erburthened with an earthly weight;
A pilgrim through the world and sky,
    Towards the Celestial Gate.


No answer wheresoe'er I roam—
    From skies afar no guiding ray;
But, hark! the voice of Christ says, " Come!
    Arise! I am the way!"
    12

# THE GREAT ARE FALLING FROM US.

The great are falling from us—to the dust
    Our flag droops midway full of many sighs;
A nation's glory and a people's trust
    Lie in the ample pall where Webster lies.

The great are falling from us—one by one
    As fall the patriarchs of the forest trees,
The winds shall seek them vainly, and the sun
    Gaze on each vacant space for centuries.

Lo, Carolina mourns her steadfast pine
   Which towered sublimely o'er the Southern realm,
And Ashland hears no more the voice divine
   From out the branches of its stately elm :—


And Marshfield's giant oak, whose stormy brow
   Oft turned the ocean tempest from the West,
Lies on the shore he guarded long—and now
   Our startled eagle knows not where to rest !

# THE DEPARTURE.

ALL around me glows the harvest
　　As I drop below the town,
And the pleasant song of workmen
　　On the breeze is floating down.

Far away the slender brooklet
　　Gleams upon the yellow plain,
Like a newly sharpened sickle
　　Dropped amid the golden grain.

By the town and through the valleys
  Sweeps the flashing river fast,
Like a herald to the future
  With a summons from the past.


Now my soul hath caught the music
  Of the happy harvest strain,
And the stream of gladness flashes,
  Like the brooklet, in my brain.


And, responsive to the river,
  How my spirit sweeps along,
As it goes to meet the future
  With a purpose firm and strong!

# A PSALM FOR THE SORROWING.

Gray wanderer in a homeless world,
    Poor pilgrim to a dusty bier;
On Time's great cycle darkly hurled
    From year to year:
See in the sky these words unfurled:
    "Thy home is here!"

Pale mourner, whose quick tears reveal
    Thy weight of sorrow but begun:
Not long thy burdened soul shall reel
    Beneath the sun;
A few swift circles of the wheel,
    And all is done

Though galled with fetters ye have lain,
    To vulture hopes and fears a prey;
Oh, moan not o'er your ceaseless pain
    Or slow decay;
For know, the soul thus files its chain
    And breaks away.

# NIGHT.

Oн Night, most beautiful and rare!
   Thou giv'st the heavens their holiest hue,
And through the azure fields of air
   Bring'st down the gentle dew.

Most glorious occupant of heaven,
   And fairest of the earth and sea,
The wonders of the sky are given,
   Imperial Night, to thee!

For thou, with angel music blest,
   Didst stand in that dim age afar,
And hold upon thy trembling breast
   Messiah's herald star!

In Olivet thou heard'st Him pray,
   And wept thy dews in softer light,
And kissed his sacred tears away,
   Thrice blessed, loving Night!

And thou didst overweigh with sleep
   The watchers at the sepulchre;
And heard'st the asking Mary weep
   Till Jesus answered her.

For this I love thy hallowed reign;
   For more than this thrice blest thou art;
Thou gain'st the unbeliever's brain
   By entering at the heart!

Oh Night, whose loving smile divine
   Thus lifts the spirit from the dust,
God's best and brightest gifts are thine—
   All thine and it is just.

# WINTER.

Sad soul—dear heart, O why repine?
The melancholy tale is plain—
The leaves of spring, the summer flowers
Have bloomed and died again.

The sweet and silver-sandalled Dew
Which like a maiden fed the flowers,
Hath waned into the beldame Frost,
And walked amid our bowers.

Some buds there were—sad hearts, be still!—
Which looked awhile unto the sky,
Then breathed but once or twice, to tell
How sweetest things may die!

And some must blight where many bloom ;—
　　But, blight or bloom, the fruit must fall !
Why sigh for spring or summer flowers,
　　Since Winter gathers all ?


He gathers all—but chide him not—
　　He wraps them in his mantle cold,
And folds them close, as best he can,
　　For he is blind and old.


Sad soul—dear heart, no more repine—
　　The tale is beautiful and plain :
Surely as Winter taketh all,
　　The Spring shall bring again.

# THE BARDS.

WHEN the sweet day in silence hath departed,
   And twilight comes with dewy, downcast eyes,
The glowing spirits of the mighty-hearted
   Like stars around me rise.

Spirits whose voices pour an endless measure,
   Exhaustless as the choral founts of night,
Until my trembling soul, oppressed with pleasure,
   Throbs in a flood of light.

Old Homer's song in mighty undulations
   Comes surging ceaseless up the oblivious main :—
I hear the rivers from succeeding nations
     Go answering down again.


Hear Virgil's strain through pleasant pastures strolling,
   And Tasso's sweeping round through Palestine,
And Dante's deep and solemn river rolling
     Through groves of midnight pine.


I hear the iron Norseman's numbers ringing
   Through frozen Norway like a herald's horn;
And like a lark, hear glorious Chaucer singing
     Away in England's morn.


In Rhenish halls, still hear the pilgrim lover
   Chant his wild story to the wailing strings,
Till the young maiden's eyes are brimming over
     Like the full cup she brings.


And hear from Scottish hills the souls unquiet
   Pouring in torrents their perpetual lays,
As their impetuous mountain runnels riot
     In the long rainy days;

The world-wide Shakspeare—the imperial Spenser:
    Whose shafts of song o'ertop the angels' seats,—
While, delicate as from a silver censer,
        Float the sweet dreams of Keats!


Nor these alone—for through the growing present,
    Westward the starry path of Poesy lies—
Her glorious spirit, like the evening crescent,
        Comes rounding up the skies.

# THE DISTANT MART.

The day is shut :—November's night,
On Newark's long and rolling height
  Falls suddenly and soon ;—
At once the myriad stars disclose ;
And in the east a glory glows
Like that the red horizon shows
  Above the moon.

But on the western mountain tops
The moon, in new-born beauty, drops
  Her pale and slender ring ;
Still, like a phantom rising red
O'er haunted valleys of the dead,
I see the distant east dispread
  Its fiery wing.

I know by thoughts, which, like the skies,
Grow darker as they slowly rise
      Above my burning heart,
It is the light the peasant views,
Through nightly falling frost and dews,
While Fancy paints in brighter hues
      The distant mart.


Through shadowy hills and meadows brown
The calm Passaic reaches down
      Where the broad waters lie;—
From hillside homes what visions teem !
The fruitless hope—ambitious dream—
Go freighted downward with the stream,
      And yonder die !


And youths and maids with strange desires
O'er quiet homes and village spires
      Behold the radiance grow;
They see the lighted casements fine—
The crowded halls of splendour shine—
The gleaming jewels and the wine—
      But not the woe !

Take from yon flaunting flame the ray
Which glows on heads untimely gray,
      On blasted heart and brain,—
From rooms of death the watcher's lamp,
From homes of toil, from hovels damp,
And dens where Shame and Crime encamp
      With Want and Pain :—

From vain bazaars and gilded halls,
Where every misnamed pleasure palls,
      Remove the chandeliers;
Then mark the scanty, scattered rays,
And think amid that dwindled blaze
How few shall walk their happy ways
      And shed no tears !

But now, when fade the fevered gleams,
*Some* trouble melts away to dreams,
      *Some* pain to sweet repose :—
And as the midnight shadows sweep,
Life's noisy torrent drops to sleep,
Its unseen current dark and deep
      In silence flows.

13

# THE TWINS.

From a beautiful lake on the mountain
    Two rivulets came down,
Prattling awhile to the violets,
    Mid shadows green and brown.

Over beds of golden lustre,
    Around by rock and tree,
They sang the same tune with their silvery tongues,
    And clapped their hands in glee.

Over rocks with mosses mantled,
  They eddied and whirled, like a waltzing pair,
Till, hand in hand, with laughter and leap
  They mingled their misty hair.


Over the self-same ledges,
  Singing the self-same tune,
They passed from April to breezy May,
  Toward the fields of June.


They whirled, and danced, and dallied,
  And through the meadows slid,
Till under the same thick grass and flowers
  Their further course was hid !


I saw two beautiful children
  Of one fair mother born,
Playing among the dewy buds
  That bloomed beneath the morn.


The same in age and beauty,
  The same in voice and size,
The same bright hair upon their necks,
  The same shade in their eyes.

Singing the same song ever
  In the self-same silvery tune,
They passed from April into May,
  Toward the fields of June.

.

They whirled, and danced, and dallied
  The beautiful vales amid,
Till under the same thick leaves and flowers
  Their future course was hid.

# LINES WRITTEN IN FLORENCE.

Within this far Etruscan clime,
　　By vine-clad slopes and olive plains,
And round these walls still left by Time,
　　The bound'ries of his old domains :—


Here at the dreamer's golden goal,
　　Whose dome o'er winding Arno drops,
Where old Romance still breathes its soul
　　Through Poesy's enchanted stops :—


Where Art still holds her ancient state
　　(What though her banner now is furled),
And keeps within her guarded gate
　　The household treasures of the world :—

What joy amid all this to find
　　One single bird, or flower, or leaf,
Earth's any simplest show designed
　　For pleasure, what though frail or brief—


If but that leaf, or bird, or flower
　　Were wafted from the western strand,
To breathe into one happy hour
　　The freshness of my native land !


That joy is mine—the bird I hear,
　　The flower is blooming near me now,
The leaf that some great bard might wear
　　In triumph on his sacred brow.


For lady, while thy voice and face
　　Make thee the Tuscan's loveliest guest,
Within this old romantic space
　　Breathes all the freshness of the West.

# A NIGHT AT THE BLACK SIGN.

Ye, who follow to the measure
    Where the trump of Fortune leads,
And at inns a-glow with pleasure
    Rein your golden-harnessed steeds,
In your hours of lordly leisure
    Have ye heard a voice of woe
On the starless wind of midnight
        Come and go?

Pilgrim brothers, whose existence
    Rides the higher roads of Time,
Hark, how from the troubled distance,
    Voices made by woe sublime,
In their sorrow, claim assistance,
    Though it come from friend or foe—
Shall they ask and find no answer?
        Rise and go.

One there was, who in his sadness
　　Laid his staff and mantle down,
Where the demons laughed to madness
　　What the night-winds could not drown—
Never came a voice of gladness
　　Though the cups should foam and flow,
And the pilgrim thus proclaiming
　　　Rose to go.


" All the night I hear the speaking
　　Of low voices round my bed,
And the dreary floor a-creaking
　　Under feet of stealthy tread :—
Like a very demon shrieking
　　Swings the black sign to and fro,
Come, arise, thou cheerless keeper,
　　　For I go.


" On the hearth the brands are lying
　　In a black, unseemly show ;
Through the roof the winds are sighing,
　　And they will not cease to blow ;
Through the house sad hearts replying
　　Send their answer deep and low—
Come, arise, thou cheerless keeper,
　　　For I go.

" Tell me not of fires relighted
    And of chambers glowing warm,
Or of travellers benighted,
    Overtaken by the storm.
Urge me not; your hand is blighted
    As your heart is—even so !
Come, arise, thou cheerless keeper—
        For I go.


" Tell me not of goblets teeming
    With the antidote of pain,
For its taste and pleasant seeming
    Only hide the deadly bane;
Hear your sleepers tortured dreaming,
    How they curse thee in their woe !
Come, arise, thou cheerless keeper,
        For I go.


" I will leave your dreary tavern
    Ere I drink its mandragore :
Like a black and hated cavern,
    There are reptiles on the floor;
They have overrun your tavern,
    They are at your wine below !
Come, arise, thou fearful keeper,
        For I go.

" There's an hostler in your stable
　　Tends a steed no man may own,
And against your windy gable
　　How the night-birds scream and moan !
Even the bread upon your table
　　Is the ashy food of woe ;
Come, arise, thou fearful keeper,
　　　　For I go.


" Here I will not seek for slumber,
　　And I will not taste your wine :
All your house the fiends encumber,
　　And they are no mates of mine ;
Never more I join your number
　　Though the tempests rain or snow—
Here's my staff and here's my mantle,
　　　　And I go."


Suffering brothers—doubly brothers—
　　(Pain hath made us more akin)
Trust not to the strength of others,
　　Trust the arm of strength within ;
One good hour of courage smothers
　　All the ills an age can know ;
Take your staff and take your mantle,
　　　　Rise and go.

# A DESERTED FARM.

The elms were old, and gnarled, and bent—
    The fields, untilled, were choked with weeds,
Where every year the thistles sent
    Wider and wider their winged seeds.

Farther and farther the nettle and dock
    Went colonizing o'er the plain,
Growing each season a plenteous stock
    Of burrs to protect their wild domain.

The last who ever had ploughed the soil
    Now in the furrowed churchyard lay—
The boy who whistled to lighten his toil
    Was a sexton somewhere far away.


Instead, you saw how the rabbit and mole
    Burrowed and furrowed with never a fear;
How the tunnelling fox looked out of his hole,
    Like one who notes if the skies are clear.


No mower was there to startle the birds
    With the noisy whet of his recking scythe;
The quail, like a cow-boy calling his herds,
    Whistled to tell that his heart was blithe.


Now all was bequeathed with pious care—
    The groves and fields fenced round with briers—
To the birds that sing in the cloisters of air,
    And the squirrels, those merry woodland friars.

# LINES TO A BIRD.



WHENCE comest thou, oh wandering soul of song?
  Round the celestial gates hast thou been winging,
And hearkening to the angels all night long
  To brighten earth with somewhat of their singing?


Thou child of sunshine, spirit of the flowers!
  Nature, through thee, with loving tongue rejoices,
Until these walls dissolve themselves to bowers,
  And all the air is full of woodland voices.


The winds that slumbered in the fields of dew,
  Float round me now with music on their pinions,
Such as I heard while yet my years were few,
  By native streams, in boyhood's lost dominions

And with the breath of morning on my brow,
 I hear the accents of the few who love me;
Sing on, full heart! I am no exile now—
 This is no foreign sky that smiles above me.


I hear the happy sounds of household glee,
 The heart's own music, floating here to bless me,
And little ones who smiled upon my knee
 Now clap the dimpled hands that would caress me.


Oh! music sweeter than the sweetest chime
 Of magic bells by fairies set a-swinging;
I am no pilgrim in a foreign clime,
 With these blest visions ever round me clinging.


I hear a voice no melody can reach;
 Dear lips, speak on in your accustomed measure,
And teach my heart what you so well can teach,
 How only love is earth's enduring pleasure.


Oh! music sweeter than the Arcadian's tune,
 Wooing the dryads from the woodlands haunted;
Or than beneath the mellow harvest moon,
 Trembles at midnight over lakes enchanted!

Oh! sweeter than the herald of the morn,
    The clarion lark, that wakes the drowsy peasant,
Is this which thrills my breast, so else forlorn,
    And with the Past and distant fills the Present.


Thus, with the music ringing in my heart,
    I may awhile forget an exile's sorrow,
And, armed with courage, rise—and so depart;
    But what sweet bird shall sing to me to-morrow ?

# THE SCULPTOR'S LAST HOUR.

*All in their lifetime carve their own soul's statue.*

Tʜᴇ middle chimes of night were dead;—
The sculptor pressed his sleepless bed,
With locks grown gray in a world of sin;
His eyes were sunken, his cheeks were thin;
And, like a leaf on a withering limb,
The fluttering life still clung to him.

While gazing on the shadowy wall,
He heard the muffled knocker fall:—
Before an answering foot could stir,
Entered the midnight messenger:

Around his shining shoulders rolled
Long and gleaming locks of gold;
The radiance of his features fell
In Beauty's light unspeakable,
And like the matin song of birds,
Swelled the rich music of his words.

" Arise ! it is your monarch's will;
Ere sounds from the imperial hill
The warder's trumpet-blast,
His palace portal must be passed :
Arise ! and be the veil withdrawn,
And let the long-wrought statue dawn !
The stars that fill the fields of light
Must pale before its purer light;
The unblemished face—the spotless limb,
Must shine among the seraphim :
Faultless in form—in nothing dim—
It must be ere it come to Him !"

The sculptor rose with heavy heart,
And slowly put the veil apart,
And stood with downcast look, entranced,
The while the messenger advanced,
And thought he heard, yet knew not why,
His hopes like boding birds go by,

And felt his heart sink ceaselessly
Down, like the friendless dead at sea.
O! for one breath to stir the air,
To break the stillness of despair;
Welcome alike, though it were given
From sulphurous shade, or vales of Heaven!

Now on the darkness swelled a sigh!—
The sculptor raised his languid eye,
And saw the radiant stranger stand
Hiding his sorrow with his hand;
His heart a billowy motion kept,
  And ever, with its fall and rise,
The stillness of the air was swept
    With a long wave of sighs.
    The old man's anxious asking eyes
    Grew larger with their blank surprise,
With wonder why he wept:—
    And while his eyes and wonder grew,—
    Came, with the tears which gushed anew,
The music of the stranger's tongue,
    But broken, like a swollen rill
    That heaves adown its native hill,
Sobbing where late it sung:—
    "Is this the statue fair and white

A long laborious life hath wrought,
And which our generous Prince hath bought?
Is this (so soulless, soiled, and dull)
  To pass the golden gates of light
And stand among the beautiful?
The lines which seam the front and cheek
Too well unholy lusts bespeak;
The brow by Anger's hand is weighed,
And Malice there his scar hath made;
There Scorn hath set her seal secure,
And curled the lip against the poor;
And Hate hath fixed the steady glance
Which Jealousy hath turned askance;
While thoughts, of those dark parents born,
Innumerable, from night till morn,
And morn till night, have wrought their will,
Like stones upon a barren hill.
Old man! although thy locks be gray,
And life's last hour is on its way—
Although thy limbs with palsy quake,
Thy hands, like windy branches, shake—
Ere from yon rampart high and round
The watchful warder's blast shall sound,
Let this be altered—still it may,—
Your Monarch brooks no more delay!"
The stranger spake and passed away.

A moment stood the aged man
  With lips apart, and looks aghast,
  Still gazing where the stranger passed.
And now a shudder o'er him ran,
As chill November's breezes sweep
  Across the dying meadow grass;
His tongue was dry, he could not speak,
  His eyes were glazed like heated glass.
But when the tears began to creep
Adown the channels of his cheek,
    A long and shadowy train,
    Born of his sorrowing brain,
With shining feet, and noiseless tread,
By dewy-eyed Repentance led,
Around the statue pressed:
With eager hand and swelling breast
Hope, jubilant, the chisel seized
  And heavenward turned the eye;
Forgiveness, radiant and pleased,
The ridges of the brow released;
  While with a tear and sigh
Sweet Charity the scorn effaced;
  And Mercy, mild and fair,
Upon the lips her chisel placed,
  And left her signet there:

And Love, the earliest born of Heaven,
  Over the features glowing, ran;
While Peace, the best and latest given,
  Finished what Hope began.


One minute now before the last,
  The stately stranger came;
A smile upon the statue cast—
Then to the fainting stranger passed,
  And spake his errand and his name:
And on the old man's latest breath
Swelled the sweet whisper, "Welcome, Death!"
  Afar from the imperial height
  Sounded the warder's horn:
  Upward, by singing angels borne,
The statue passed the gates of light
Outshining all the stars of night,
  And fairer than the morn.

# THE SCULPTOR'S FUNERAL.

Through the darkened streets of Florence,
Moving toward thy church, Saint Lorenz,
Marched the bearers, masked and singing,
With their ghostly flambeaux flinging
Ghostlier shadows that went winging
Round the portals and the porches,
As if spirits, which had hovered
In the darkness undiscovered,
Danced about the hissing torches,
Like the moths that whirl and caper
Drunken round an evening taper.

Unconsoled and unconsoling
Rolled the Arno, louder rolling
As the rain poured—and the tolling,
Though the thick shower fell demurely,
Fell from out one turret only
Where the bell swung sad and lonely
Prisoned in the cloud securely.
Masked in black, with voices solemn
Strode the melancholy column,
With a stiff and soulless burden
Bearing to the grave its guerdon,
While the torch flames, vexed and taunted
By the night winds, leapt and flaunted,
Mid the funeral rains that slanted,
Those brave bearers marched and chanted,
Through the darkness thick and dreary,
With a woful voice and weary,

MISERERE.

Light to light and dark to dark,
  Kindred natures thus agree;
Where the soul soars none can mark,
But the world below may hark—
  *Miserere, Domine!*

Dew to dew, and rain to rain,
  Swell the streams and reach the sea;
When the drouth shall burn the plain,
Then the sands shall but remain—
  *Miserere, Domine.*


Flame to flame—let ashes fall
  Where the fireless ashes be;
Embers black and funeral
Unto dying cinders call—
  *Miserere, Domine!*


Life to life and dust to dust!
  Christ, who died upon the tree,
Thine the promise, ours the trust,
We are weak—but thou art just—
  *Miserere, Domine!*


### FIRST BYSTANDER.

There, stand aside, the very eaves are weeping
As are the heavens in sympathy with us :—
Italia's air hath not within its keeping
A nobler heart than that which lies there sleeping,
For whom the elements are wailing thus.

SECOND BYSTANDER.

I reverenced him—he was a marvellous schemer;
Hath built more airy structures in his day
Than ever wild and opiate-breathing dreamer
Hath drugged his dreams with even in Cathay.
His fancy went in marble round the earth
And whitened it with statues—where he trod
The silent people leapt to sudden birth,
And all the sky, exulting high and broad,
Became a mighty Pantheon for God.


THIRD BYSTANDER.

You reverenced him?  I loved him, with a scope
Of feeling I may never know again;
And love him still, even though beyond all hope
The priest, the bishop, cardinal, and pope,
Should banish him to wear a burning chain
In those great dungeons of the unforgiven,
Under the space-deep castle walls of Heaven.
I know the Church considered it a sin,
I know the Duke considered it a shame—
That our Alzoni would not stoop to win
What any blunderer, now-a-day, may claim,
A niche in Santa Croce,—which hath been,
And is, to them, the very shrine of Fame!

Why, look you, why should one carve out his soul
In bits to meet the world's unthankful stare;
For Ignorance to hold in his control
And sly-eyed Jealousy's detracting glare?
To see the golden glories of his brain
Out-glittered by a brazen counterfeit?
The starriest spirit only shines in vain,
When every rocket can outdazzle it!


CHORUS OF STUDENTS, FOLLOWING.

They bear the great Alzoni—he is dead,—
 Our hope is dead, and lies on yonder bier;
 There is no comfort left for any here
   Since he is dead.


Oh, mother Florence, droop your queenly head,
 And mingle ashes with your wreath of flowers—
 Build funeral altars in your ducal bowers;
   For he is dead.


Oh, sacred Arno, be your ripples shed
 No more in music o'er your silver sands,
 But mourn to death, and wring your watery hands;
   For he is dead.

Ye dusky palaces, whose gloom is wed
    To princely names that never may depart,
    Drown all your lights in tears—the prince of Art,
        Your hope, is dead !


Ye spirits who to glory have been led,
    In years agone, departed souls of might,
    Make joyful space in Heaven, for our delight
        On earth is dead.


———


And thus with melancholy songs they bore him
    Into the chapel—'twixt the columns vast
They set the bier, and lit great tapers o'er him,
        And looked their last.


They looked and pondered on his dreamy history
    Whose sudden close had left them broken-hearted,
Till cloudy censers veiled the light in mystery,
        And they departed.

# DOOMED AND FORGOTTEN.

Two mighty angels in the outer blue,
    With great palm branches slanting in their hands,
Stood by the golden gate that guards the view
    Wherein God's temple stands.


So still they were, the porphyry pillars high
    That propt the fretted cornice and the frieze,
Stood not more breathless when the choral sky
    Withheld its symphonies.

And golden haloes bound their brows in light,
   Till each head shone like Saturn with his rings,
And to their sandals, beautiful and bright
   Went down their crosswise wings.


Low at their feet, with pinions all distraught,
   As they the Siroc's stormy path had swept,
And ashen cheeks still hot with burning thought,
   A spirit sat and wept :—


And shed such tears as from the heart can flow
   Alone when Hope flies far from our distress,
Leaving no guide athwart the world of woe,
   The pathless wilderness.


Thus have I seen some sad and sightless one,
   Before a palace with nor hound nor staff,
Sit weeping in the sultry dust, with none
   To speak in his behalf.


But happier far that prisoner from the day,
   With all the sunlight mocking his blank eyes,
Than him, whose doomèd path forgotten lay
   Along the under skies.

Doomed and forgotten ! These are sounds attuned
  To all the world conceives of misery—
And drown the heart, as if the last wave swooned
  Above us in the sea !


Doomed and forgotten—by our God forgot,
  Who noteth even the sparrow in his fall;
With whom the smallest living thing is not
  For his great care too small.


Doomed and forgotten—at the angel's feet
  He sat with dull and weary wings deprest,—
But now, where once the song of peace was sweet,
  There came no voice of rest.


There was a time, while yet his cheek's soft glow
  Bloomed in the boyhood of his earthly years,
He had a vision, which no man may know,
  That drowned his eyes with tears.


Some God-sent angel, wavering down the sky,
  Had sought him when the world was most apart,
And given this vision to his dreaming eye,
  And stamped it on his heart.

Then he withdrew from all his fellow youths,
His heaven-touched soul with inspiration filled,
And said "My time is God's; the cause is Truth's;
Beneath their dome I build!"


For days and nights he walked the solemn wood,
Rounding to fullest form his great intent,
And viewless phantoms all about him stood,
And followed where he went.


If he despaired, the pine-cone in his way
Fell from the limb that sentinels the wind—
The small spring whispered courage where it lay
In ancient rocks enshrined.


The wintry mountain stood with glory topt,
And Iris bound the labouring torrent's brow,
The acorn, full of future summers, dropt
From out the stormy bough.


The flowery vines in Nature's unseen hand
Curled into wreaths, as if Fame wandered there,—
The laurel, leaning o'er the pathway, fanned
The brightness of his hair.

There was a time !—oh, sad and bitter breath
    That sighs o'er loss of days, no more to be—
Of actions dropt to dreams—and dreams to death,
    And then—Eternity !


There crouched the spirit, abject and forlorn,
    Upon the azure highway, like a blot,
And raised its low voice, for they needs must mourn
    The doomed and the forgot.


But soon, abashed to hear his own "alas !"
    He took his way aslant the nether space—
And, wheresoe'er a star beheld him pass,
    It turned and veiled its face !


Oh soul, remember, howe'er small the scope
    Of thought, or action, that around thee lies,
It is the finished task alone can ope
    The gates of Paradise.

# SONG OF THE ALPINE GUIDE.

On Zurich's spires, with rosy light,
  The mountains smile at morn and eve,
And Zurich's waters, blue and bright,
  The glories of those hills receive.
And there my sister trims her sail,
  That like a wayward swallow flies;
But I would rather meet the gale
  That fans the eagle in the skies.

She sings in Zurich's chapel choir,
  Where rolls the organ on the air,
And bells proclaim, from spire to spire,
  Their universal call to prayer.
  15

But let me hear the mountain rills,
  And old Saint Bernard's storm-bell toll,
And, mid these great cathedral hills,
  The thundering avalanches roll.

My brother wears a martial plume,
  And serves within a distant land,—
The flowers that on his bosom bloom
  Are placed there by a stranger hand.
Love meets him but in foreign eyes,
  And greets him in a foreign speech :—
But she who to my heart replies
  Must speak the tongue these mountains teach.

The warrior's trumpet o'er him swells,
  The triumph which it only hath ;
But let me hear the mule-worn bells
  Speak peace in every mountain path.
His spear is ever 'gainst a foe,
  Where waves the hostile flag abroad ;—
My pike-staff only cleaves the snow,
  My banner the blue sky of God.

On Zurich's side my mother sits,
  And to her whirring spindle sings—
Through Zurich's wave my father's nets
  Sweep daily with their filmy wings.

To that beloved voice I list
   And view that father's toil with pride;
But, like a low and vale-born mist,
   My spirit climbs the mountain side.


And I would ever hear the stir
   And turmoil of the singing winds,
Whose viewless wheels around me whirr,
   Whose distaffs are the swaying pines.
And, on some snowy mountain head,
   The deepest joy to me is given,
When, net-like, the great storm is spread
   To sweep the azure lake of heaven.


Then, since the vale delights me not,
   And Zurich woos in vain below,
And it hath been my joy and lot
   To scale these Alpine crags of snow—
And since in life I loved them well,
   Let me in death lie down with them,
And let the pines and tempests swell
   Around me their great requiem.

# MORNING IN MARTIGNY.

'Tis sunrise on Saint Bernard's snow,
'Tis dawn within the vale below;
And in Martigny's streets appear
The mule and noisy muleteer;
And tinklings fill the rosy air,
Until the mountain pass seems there,
Up whose steep pathway scarcely stirs
The long, slow line of travellers;
And in the shadowy town is heard
The sound of many a foreign word.

Old men are there, whose locks are white
As yonder cloud which veils the height;
And maidens, whose young cheeks are kissed
  By ringlets flashing bright or dark,

Whose hearts are light as yonder mist
  That holds the music of the lark—
And youths are there with jest and laugh,
Each bearing his oft-branded staff
To chronicle, when all is done,
The dangerous heights his feet have won.


So toils through life the pilgrim soul
  Mid rocky ways and valleys fair;
At every base or glorious goal,
  His staff receives the record there—
The names that shall for ever twine,
And blossom like a fragrant vine—
Or, like a serpent, round it cling
Eternally to coil and sting.

# A MAIDEN'S TEARS.

O, WHEN a maiden's soul is stirred
　　To pity's deepest, last excess,
And, like some lonely, brooding bird,
　　Folds its bright wings in mournfulness;
And pours its sympathy in sighs,
　　That sweeten on the rosy lips;
And sends the tears into the eyes,
　　To flood them with a half eclipse,—
How brighter its veiled beauty shows
Than all the light which joy bestows!

Thus fairer the fair flower appears,
　Beneath a dewy fullness bowed;
The moon a double lustre wears,
　Within the halo of a cloud.
The music of a maiden's mirth
May be the sweetest sound to earth;
But tears, in love and pity given,
Are welcomer, by far, to Heaven.

# WOMAN.

An angel wandering out of heaven,
And all too bright for Eden even,
Once through the paths of paradise
  Made luminous the auroral air;
And, walking in His awful guise,
  Met the Eternal Father there;
Who, when he saw the truant sprite,
Smiled love through all those bowers of light.
While deep within his trancèd spell,
  Our Eden sire lay slumbering near,
God saw, and said: " It is not well
  For man alone to linger here."

Then took that angel by the hand,
    And with a kiss its brow He prest,
And whispering all His mild command,
    He laid it on the sleeper's breast;
With earth enough to make it human,
He chained its wings, and called it WOMAN.
And if perchance some stains of rust
    Upon her pinions yet remain,
'Tis but the mark of God's own dust,
    The earth-mould of that Eden chain!

# THE CITY OF GOD.

" Heaven lies about us in our infancy."—Wordsworth

Ere the rose and the roseate hues of the dawn,
With the dews of my youth, were all scattered and gone;
Ere the cloud, like the far reaching wing of the night,
Had shut out the glory of God from my sight,
I saw a wide realm in the azure unfold,
Where the fields nodded towards me their flowers of gold;
And the soft airs sailed o'er them, and dropt from above,
As if shed from innumerous pinions of love:

There were trees with broad boles steeped in perfume and
    dew,
While their full breasts for ever leaned up to the blue—
And within their wide bosoms the winds seemed to rest
With the calm like the sleep of a soul that is blest;
Or, if any light rustle stole out from their limbs,
'Twas the murmurous music of delicate hymns—
As if some dear angel sat singing within
To a spirit just won from the regions of sin:
There were streams which seemed born but in slumberous
    bowers,
Stealing down, like a dream, through the sleep of the
    flowers—
So pure was the azure they won from the height,
The blue hills seemed melting to rivers of light;
And within this fair realm, where but angels have trod,
I beheld, as I thought, the great CITY OF GOD!
All its high walls were pierced with no engines of Death—
No moat, with its dull pool, lay stagnant beneath:
The last bolts, I ween, the stout heart has to fear,
Are pointed and sped from Death's citadel here;
And the last hungry moat the pure soul has to brave,
Ere it passes the portal to bliss, is the grave!
There the wide wall went East till it dimmed to the view—
And the wide wall went West till it passed into blue;

And the broad gates stood open, inviting that way,
Like the hands of the Lord to his children astray.
There were high towers, climbing still dazzingly higher,
Till each shone like a fixed guiding pillar of fire;
And the angels who watched on their summits afar,
So lessened by distance, gleamed each as a star:
And the great dome that templed the Father in light,
Seemed to swell and to circle and swell on the sight—
As some angel who cleaves his bright way 'mid the
    spheres,
Beholds the blue dome of the earth as he nears.
There was music—my soul unto memory yields,
And hears the low sounds floating over the fields—
But, alas! not as then, with its rapturous desire—
Like some bird that sits hushed by the song of a choir;
It melted and flowed o'er the walls and the towers,
And sweet as if breathed from the lips of the flowers—
As if the bright blossoms, with loving accord,
Had risen and sang to the praise of the Lord!
Then I thought 'mid that music to wander and wait
For the loved ones, just there by the palm at the gate,
To begin the great life that no Death can o'ertake,
And to dream the great dream that no tumult can break;
In the broad world of Beauty, of flowers and bliss—
But, alas! I awoke where the thorns grow in this:

And the walls of Death's citadel now intervene,
And the grave, like a moat, yawns here darkly between:
But still, through the mists and the shadows of night,
I can follow the stars on those pillars of light;
And I know the great gates stand there open and broad,
Inviting the way to the *City of God.*

# THE TRUANT.

Where is the truant?   This should be the place,
  Where even now we heard him laugh outright,
To greet the sun, as if he saw the face
  Of some bright angel smiling in the light.

Surely the morn hath beckoned him away,
  Enticing him with glory from afar :
Arise ! and we may find him in his play,
  Shining amid the sweetest flowers that are.

His little eyes, so full of bright desires,
  Could not withstand yon orient space of flowers ;
And he hath 'scaped the intervening briers,
  The field for bleeding feet which we call ours.

It cannot be he wandered out alone;
  O, rather that dear friend of many charms,
Who wooed him in each light that round us shone,
  Won him at last into his careful arms.


O! look again, a little further look,
  And weep no tear unless it be for joy,
Toward yon sweet field, where flower, and bird, and brook
  Beguile the glad heart of our truant boy.


Look closer still, until your gaze has won
  And passed the barriers overflowered with stars,—
Those morning-glories closing in the sun,
  And you shall see him through the golden bars.


Watch where he goes, still making toward the light,
  Our angel truant gladly nearing home,
While a deep voice from that celestial height
  Bids us be calm and suffer him to come.

# RUTH.


SUGGESTED BY A STATUE EXECUTED BY MR. ROGERS IN
FLORENCE.


FROM age to age, from clime to clime,
  A spirit, bright as her own morn,
She walks the golden fields of Time,
  As erst amid the yellow corn.


A form o'er which the hallowed veil
  Of years bequeaths a lovelier light,
As when the mists of morning sail
  Round some far isle to make it bright.

And as some reaper 'mid the grain,
  Or binder resting o'er his sheaf,
Beheld her on the orient plain,
  A passing vision bright and brief;—


And while he gazed let fall perchance
  The sheaf or sickle from his hand—
Thus even here, as in a trance,
  Before her kneeling form I stand.


But not as then she comes and goes
  To live in memory alone;
The perfect soul before me glows
  Immortal in the living stone.


And while upon her face I gaze
  And scan her rarely rounded form,
The glory of her native days
  Comes floating o'er me soft and warm;—


Comes floating, till this shadowy place
  Brightens to noontide, and receives
The breath of that old harvest space,
  With all its sunshine and its sheaves!
16

# THE MARSEILLAISE.

I HEARD, as in a glorious dream,
   A clarion thrill the startled air,
And saw an answering people stream
   Through every noisy thoroughfare.
There were the old, whose hairs were few,
   Or white with memory of the days
Of Egypt, Moscow, Waterloo,—
   And now they sang the "*Marseillaise.*"

The aged scholar, pale and wan,
   Was there within the marshalled line,
And, jostled by the noisy van,
   The poet with his voice divine :—

No more could tomes the sage beguile;
    The bard no longer wooed the praise
That dribbles from a monarch's smile,
    For now they sang the " *Marseillaise!*"


And there were matrons, who of yore
    Had wept a son or husband slain,
Or chanted for their Emperor
    A long and loud triumphal strain :—
Their woe inspired the song no more,
    Nor yet Napoleon's crown of bays,
Which rankly sprang from fields of gore,
    For now they sang the " *Marseillaise!*"


The peasants, from their hills of vines,
    Came streaming to the open plains;
No more they bore their tax of wines
    To stagnate in a tyrant's veins;
France needed not the purple flood
    To set her heart and brain ablaze,—
A wilder wine was in her blood,
    For now she sang the " *Marseillaise!*"

The Bourbon's throne was trampled down,
 And France no longer knelt; but now,
Struck with a patriot's hand the crown
 From off the Orleans' dotard brow;—
Released from slavery and tears,
 She rose and sang fair Freedom's praise,
Till far along the future years
 I heard the swelling "*Marseillaise!*"

# THE OLD YEAR.


Lo, now, when dark December's gathering storm
With heavy wing o'ershadows many a heart,
Beside us the old year, with mailèd form,
    Stands waiting to depart.

Weighed down as with a ponderous tale of woe,
How dim his eyes, how wan his cheeks appear!
Like Denmark's spectre king, with motion slow
    He beckons the young year.

# A NIGHT THOUGHT.

Long have I gazed upon all lovely things,
　　Until my soul was melted into song,—
Melted with love, till from its thousand springs
　　The stream of adoration, swift and strong,
Swept in its ardour, drowning brain and tongue,
Till what I most would say was borne away unsung.


The brook is silent when it mirrors most
　　Whate'er is grand or beautiful above;
The billow which would woo the flowery coast
　　Dies in the first expression of its love;

And could the bard consign to living breath
Feelings too deep for thought, the utterance were death!


The starless heavens at noon are a delight;
　The clouds a wonder in their varying play,
And beautiful when from their mountainous height
　The lightning's hand illumes the wall of day :—
The noisy storm bursts down, and passing brings
The rainbow poised in air on unsubstantial wings.


But most I love the melancholy night—
　When with fixed gaze I single out a star,
A feeling floods me with a tender light—
　A sense of an existence from afar,
A life in other spheres of love and bliss,
Communion of true souls—a loneliness in this!


There is a sadness in the midnight sky—
　An answering fulness in the heart and brain,
Which tells the spirit's vain attempt to fly,
　And occupy those distant worlds again.
At such an hour Death's were a loving trust,
If life could then depart in its contempt of dust.

It may be that this deep and longing sense
　　Is but the prophecy of life to come;
It may be that the soul in going hence
　　May find in some bright star its promised home;
And that the Eden lost for ever here
Smiles welcome to me now from yon suspended sphere.


There is a wisdom in the light of stars,
　　A worldless lore which summons me away;
This ignorance belongs to earth, which bars
　　The spirit in these darkened walls of clay,
And stifles all the soul's aspiring breath;—
True knowledge only dawns within the gates of Death.


Imprisoned thus, why fear we then to meet
　　The angel who shall ope the dungeon door,
And break these galling fetters from our feet,
　　To lead us up from Time's benighted shore?
Is it for love of this dark cell of dust,
Which, tenantless, awakes but horror and disgust?


Long have I mused upon all lovely things;
　　But thou, oh Death! art lovelier than all;

Thou sheddest from thy recompensing wings
  A glory which is hidden by the pall—
The excess of radiance falling from thy plume
Throws from the gates of Time a shadow on the tomb

# SONG OF THE SERF.

I know a lofty lady,
  And she is wondrous fair;
She hath wrought my soul to music
  As the leaves are wrought by air;
And like the air that wakes
  The foliage into play,
She feels no thrill of all she makes
  When she has passed away.

I know a lofty lady
  Who seldom looks on me,
Or when she smiles, her smile is like
  The moon's upon the sea.

As proudly and serene
  She shines from her domain,
Till my spirit heaves beneath her mien,
  And floods my aching brain.


I know a lofty lady :—
  But I would not wake her scorn
By telling all the love I bear,
  For I am lowly born ;
*So* low, and she *so* high—
  And the space between us spread
Makes me but as the weeds that lie
  Beneath her stately tread.

# BALBOA.


From San Domingo's crowded wharf
   Fernandez' vessel bore,
To seek in unknown lands afar
   The Indian's golden ore.


And hid among the freighted casks,
   Where none might see or know,
Was one of Spain's immortal men,
   Three hundred years ago!

But when the fading town and land
  Had dropped below the sea,
He met the captain face to face,
  And not a fear had he!


"What villain thou?" Fernandez cried,
  "And wherefore serve us so?"
"To be thy follower," he replied
  Three hundred years ago.


He wore a manly form and face,
  A courage firm and bold,
His words fell on his comrades' hearts,
  Like precious drops of gold.


They saw not his ambitious soul;
  He spoke it not—for lo!
He stood among the common ranks
  Three hundred years ago.


But when Fernandez' vessel lay
  At golden Darien,
A murmur, born of discontent,
  Grew loud among the men:

And with the word there came the act;
  And with the sudden blow
They raised Balboa from the ranks,
  Three hundred years ago.


And while he took command beneath
  The banner of his lord,
A mighty purpose grasped his soul,
  As he had grasped the sword.


He saw the mountain's fair blue height
  Whence golden waters flow;
Then with his men he scaled the crags,
  Three hundred years ago.


He led them up through tangled brakes,
  The rivulet's sliding bed,
And through the storm of poisoned darts
  From many an ambush shed.


He gained the turret crag—alone—
  And wept! to see below,
An ocean, boundless and unknown.
  Three hundred years ago.

And while he raised upon that height
  The banner of his lord,
The mighty purpose grasped him still,
  As still he grasped his sword.


Then down he rushed with all his men,
  As headlong rivers flow,
And plunged breast-deep into the sea,
  Three hundred years ago.


And while he held above his head
  The conquering flag of Spain,
He waved his gleaming sword, and smote
  The waters of the main:


For Rome! for Leon! and Castile!
  Thrice gave the cleaving blow;
And thus Balboa claimed the sea,
  Three hundred years ago.

# LABOUR.

" Labour, labour !" sounds the anvil,
  " Labour, labour, until death !"
And the file, with voice discordant,
  " Labour, endless labour !" saith.
While the bellows to the embers
  Speak of labour in each breath.

" Labour, labour !" in the harvest,
  Saith the whetting of the scythe,
And the mill-wheel tells of labour
  Under waters falling blithe;
"Labour, labour !" groaned the millstones,
  To the bands that whirl and writhe;

And the woodman tells of labour,
  In his echo-waking blows;
In the forest, in the cabin,
  'Tis the dearest word he knows.
"Labour, labour!" saith the spirit,
  And with labour comes repose.

"Labour!" saith the loaded wagon,
  Moving towards the distant mart.
"Labour!" groans the heavy steamer,
  As she cleaves the waves apart.
Beating like that iron engine,
  "Labour, labour!" cries the heart.

Yes, the heart of man cries "labour!'
  While it labours in the breast.
But the Ancient and Eternal,
  In the Word which he hath blest,
Sayeth, "Six days shalt thou labour,
  On the seventh thou shalt rest!"

Then how beautiful at evening,
  When the toilsome week is done,
To behold the blacksmith's anvil
  Die in darkness with the sun;
And to think the doors of labour
  Are all closing up like one.
  17

# THE WINDY NIGHT.


ALOW and aloof,
Over the roof,
How the midnight tempests howl!
With a dreary voice, like the dismal tune
Of wolves that bay at the desert moon;—
Or whistle and shriek
Through limbs that creak,
"Tu-who! tu-whit!"
They cry and flit,
"Tu-whit! tu-who!" like the solemn owl!

Alow and aloof,
Over the roof,
Sweep the moaning winds amain,

And wildly dash
The elm and ash,
Clattering on the window-sash,
With a clatter and patter,
Like hail and rain
That well nigh shatter
The dusky pane!


Alow and aloof
Over the roof,
How the tempests swell and roar!
Though no foot is astir,
Though the cat and the cur
Lie dozing along the kitchen floor,
There are feet of air
On every stair!
Through every hall—
Through each gusty door,
There's a jostle and bustle,
With a silken rustle,
Like the meeting of guests at a festival!


Alow and aloof,
Over the roof,
How the stormy tempests swell!

And make the vane
On the spire complain—
They heave at the steeple with might and main
And burst and sweep
Into the belfry, on the bell!
They smite it so hard, and they smite it so well,
That the sexton tosses his arms in sleep,
And dreams he is ringing a funeral knell!

# A DIRGE FOR A DEAD BIRD.

The cage hangs at the window,
　There's the sunshine on the sill;
But where the form and where the voice
　That never till now were still?

The sweet voice hath departed
　From its feathery home of gold,
The little form of yellow dust
　Lies motionless and cold!

Oh, where amid the azure
　Hath thy sweet spirit fled?
I hold my breath and think I hear
　Its music overhead.

Death has not hushed thy spirit,
 Its joy shall vanish never;
The slightest thrill of pleasure born
 Lives on and lives for ever!

Throughout the gloomy winter
 Thy soul shed joy in ours,
As it told us of the summer-time
 Amid the land of flowers.

But now thy songs are silent,
 Except what memory brings;
For thou hast folded death within
 The glory of thy wings!

And here thy resting-place shall be
 Beneath the garden bower;
A bush shall be thy monument,
 Thy epitaph a flower!

# THE WITHERING LEAVES.

The summer is gone and the autumn is here,
And the flowers are strewing their earthly bier;
A dreary mist o'er the woodland swims,
While rattle the nuts from the windy limbs:
From bough to bough the squirrels run
At the noise of the hunter's echoing gun,
And the partridge flies where my footstep heaves
The rustling drifts of the withering leaves.

The flocks pursue their southern flight—
Some all the day and some all night;
And up from the wooded marshes come
The sounds of the pheasant's feathery drum.

On the highest bough the mourner crow
Sits in his funeral suit of woe :
All nature mourns—and my spirit grieves
At the noise of my feet in the withering leaves.


Oh ! I sigh for the days that have passed away,
When my life like the year had its season of May ;
When the world was all sunshine and beauty and truth,
And the dew bathed my feet in the valley of youth !
Then my heart felt its wings, and no bird of the sky
Sang over the flowers more joyous than I.
But Youth is a fable, and Beauty deceives ;—
For my footsteps are loud in the withering leaves.


And I sigh for the time when the reapers at morn
Came down from the hill at the sound of the horn :
Or when dragging the rake, I followed them out
While they tossed the light sheaves with their laughter
        about ;
Through the field, with boy-daring, barefooted I ran ;
But the stubbles foreshadowed the path of the man.
Now the uplands of life lie all barren of sheaves—
While my footsteps are loud in the withering leaves !

# THE CLOSING SCENE.

WITHIN his sober realm of leafless trees
    The russet year inhaled the dreamy air;
Like some tanned reaper in his hour of ease,
    When all the fields are lying brown and bare.

The gray barns looking from their hazy hills
    O'er the dim waters widening in the vales,
Sent down the air a greeting to the mills,
    On the dull thunder of alternate flails.

All sights were mellowed and all sounds subdued,
    The hills seemed farther and the streams sang low;
As in a dream the distant woodman hewed
    His winter log with many a muffled blow.

The embattled forests, erewhile armed in gold,
  Their banners bright with every martial hue,
Now stood, like some sad beaten host of old,
  Withdrawn afar in Time's remotest blue.


On slumbrous wings the vulture held his flight;
  The dove scarce heard his sighing mate's complaint;
And like a star slow drowning in the light,
  The village church-vane seemed to pale and faint.


The sentinel-cock upon the hill-side crew—
  Crew thrice, and all was stiller than before,—
Silent till some replying warder blew
  His alien horn, and then was heard no more.


Where erst the jay, within the elm's tall crest,
  Made garrulous trouble round her unfledged young,
And where the oriole hung her swaying nest,
  By every light wind like a censer swung:—


Where sang the noisy masons of the eaves,
  The busy swallows, circling ever near,
Foreboding, as the rustic mind believes,
  An early harvest and a plenteous year;—

Where every bird which charmed the vernal feast,
  Shook the sweet slumber from its wings at morn,
To warn the reaper of the rosy east,—
  All now was songless, empty, and forlorn.


Alone from out the stubble piped the quail,
  And croaked the crow through all the dreamy gloom;
Alone the pheasant, drumming in the vale,
  Made echo to the distant cottage loom.


There was no bud, no bloom upon the bowers;
  The spiders wove their thin shrouds night by night;
The thistle-down, the only ghost of flowers,
  Sailed slowly by, passed noiseless out of sight.


Amid all this, in this most cheerless air,
  And where the woodbine shed upon the porch
Its crimson leaves, as if the Year stood there
  Firing the floor with his inverted torch;—


Amid all this, the centre of the scene,
  The white-haired matron, with monotonous tread,
Plied the swift wheel, and with her joyless mien,
  Sat, like a Fate, and watched the flying thread.

She had known Sorrow,—he had walked with her,
  . Oft supped and broke the bitter ashen crust;
And in the dead leaves still she heard the stir
  Of his black mantle trailing in the dust.


While yet her cheek was bright with summer bloom,
  Her country summoned and she gave her all;
And twice War bowed to her his sable plume—
  Regave the swords to rust upon her wall.


Regave the swords,—but not the hand that drew
  And struck for Liberty its dying blow,
Nor him who, to his sire and country true,
  Fell 'mid the ranks of the invading foe.


Long, but not loud, the droning wheel went on,
  Like the low murmur of a hive at noon;
Long, but not loud, the memory of the gone
  Breathed through her lips a sad and tremulous tune.


At last the thread was snapped—her head was bowed;
  Life dropped the distaff through his hands serene,—
And loving neighbours smoothed her careful shroud,
  While Death and Winter closed the autumn scene.

# THE PILGRIM TO THE LAND OF SONG.


The dews are dry upon my sandal-shoon
    Which bathed them on the foreign hills of song,
And now beneath the white and sultry noon
    They print the dust which they may wear too long.


The flowers by delicate fingers wove at morn
    Around my pilgrim staff have paled and died,
Or dropped into the sand, and lie forlorn,
    Mute orphans of the airy mountain side.

The mingled music in the early gale,
   Of bees and birds, and maidens among flowers,
The brooks, like shepherds, piping down the vale,
   For these my heart remounts the morning hours.


Oh, that I might reclimb the dewy dawn,
   And with the stars sit down by Castalie,
And be once more within the shade withdrawn,
   Mantled with music and with Poesy.


Thou blessed bird between me and the heaven,
   Thou wingèd censer, swinging through the air
With incense of pure song,—how hast thou driven
   One to the past, that may not linger there!


Oh, for one wild annihilating hour,
   Spent with the minstrels of a loftier time;
Those giants among bards, whose high songs tower
   Full many a rood o'er all our new sublime.


Oh, for an hour with Chaucer, the divine,
   The morning star of English song confessed;
Ushering a day whose slow but sure decline
   Fades with a fitful glimmering in the west.

Oh, for that rare auroral time, which brought
  The light of Shakespeare, and the glorious few,
Who, in their glowing robes of deathless thought,
  Strode knee-deep through Parnassian flowers and dew.


The hot sands gleam around me, and I thirst,—
  The wayside springs have sunk into themselves;
And even the little blossoms which they nursed,
  Have vanished from their side, like faithless elves.


Whence lead the sandy courses of these rills?
  Do they foretell a mightier stream at hand,
With voice triumphant, worthy of these hills?
  Where are thy rivers, oh, my native land?


A few brave souls have sparkled into sight,
  With living flashes of celestial art;
Souls who might flood the world with new delight,
  Keep sealed the deepest fountains of the heart.


Oh, for a cloud to oversweep the west,
  And with a deluge burst these deeper springs,—
A voiceful cloud, with grandeur in its breast,
  And lightning on its far impending wings.

Oh, for one mighty heart and fearless hand !
　For such, methinks, my country, is thy due,—
The embodied spirit of his forest land,
　Who, scorning not the old, shall sing the new.


Here will I rest until the day declines,
　A voiceless pilgrim toward the land of song;
And, like a sentinel, catch the herald signs
　Of him whose coming hath been stayed too long.

# A CUP OF WINE TO THE OLD YEAR.

**I.**

Come hither, love, come hither,
And sit you down by me;
And hither run, my little one,
And climb upon my knee.
But bring the flagon first, my love,
And fill to friends and foes,
And let the old year dash his beard
With wine before he goes.

18

II.

Oh, do you not remember
　　The night we let him in,
The creaking signs, the windy blinds,
　　The universal din;—
The melancholy sounds which bade
　　The poor old year adieu;
The sudden clamour and the bells
　　That welcomed in the new?
He brought to us a world of hope
　　Beneath his robe of snows:—
Then let the old year dash his beard
　　With wine before he goes.


III.

Oh, then the year was young and fair,
　　And loved all joyful things;
And under his bright mantle hid
　　The warning of his wings.
And you remember how the Spring
　　Beguiled him to her bowers;—
How Summer next exalted him
　　Unto her throne of flowers;—

And how the reaper, Autumn, crowned
   Him 'mid the sheaves and shocks,—
You still may see the tangled straws
   In his disordered locks.
The yellow wheat, the crimson leaves,
   With purple grapes, were there;
Till, Bacchus-like, he wore the proof
   Of plenty 'mid his hair—
A proof that wooes in harvest-homes
   Brown Labour to repose :—
Then let the old year dash his beard
   With wine before he goes.

IV.

But soon the Winter came and took
   His glory quite away :
A frosty rime o'erspread his chin,
   And all his hair went gray ;
His crown has fallen to his feet,
   And withers where he stands,
While some invisible horror shakes
   The old man by the hands.

Oh, woo him from his cloud of grief
And from his dream of woes;
And bid the old year dash his beard
With wine before he goes.


V.


For he hath brought us some new friends,
And made the old more dear;
And shown how love may constant prove,
And friendship be sincere.
Though it may be some venomed tooth
Hath wrought against the file;
And though perchance a Janus' face
Hath cursed us with its smile:—
Come, fill the goblet till its rim
With Lethe overflows;
The year shall drown their memory
With wine before he goes.


VI.


But hark! a music nears and nears,—
As if the singing stars
Were driving closer to the earth
In their triumphal cars!

And hark! the sudden pealing crash
  Of one who will not wait,
But flings into the ringing dark
  Old Winter's crystal gate.
A sigh is on the midnight air,—
  A ghost is on the lawn,—
The broken goblet strews the floor,—
  The poor old year is gone!

# THE AWAKENING YEAR.

The blue-birds and the violets
  Are with us once again,
And promises of summer spot
  The hill-side and the plain.

The clouds around the mountain tops
  Are riding on the breeze,
Their trailing azure trains of mist
  Are tangled in the trees.

The snow-drifts, which have lain so long,
  Haunting the hidden nooks,
Like guilty ghosts have slipped away,
  Unseen, into the brooks.

The streams are fed with generous rains,
   They drink the wayside springs,
And flutter down from crag to crag,
   Upon their foamy wings.


Through all the long wet nights they brawl,
   By mountain homes remote,
Till woodmen in their sleep behold
   Their ample rafts afloat.


The lazy wheel that hung so dry
   Above the idle stream,
Whirls wildly in the misty dark,
   And through the miller's dream.


Loud torrent unto torrent calls,
   Till at the mountain's feet,
Flashing afar their spectral light,
   The noisy waters meet.


They meet, and through the lowlands sweep,
   Toward briny bay and lake,
Proclaiming to the distant towns
   "The country is awake!"

# PROLOGUE TO AN UNPUBLISHED SERIO-COMIC POEM.

INSCRIBED TO GEO. H. BOKER.

I.

DEAR friend, while now the dews are shed
    Along the vintage crownèd Rhine;
And day departs with purple tread,
    Fresh dripping from the land of wine:

Here, o'er a flask of Rudesheim,
    Your shade with me shall drain the bowl,
While in this passing cup of rhyme
    I pour the fulness of my soul.

And you shall drain as I have drained
    The golden goblet of your song,
Till in my heart a pleasure reigned,
    Like Bacchus 'mid his wreathèd throng.

## II.

And blame me not, that while she sings
 My Muse not always strives to soar,—
If, folding her o'erwearied wings,
 She warbles when her flight is o'er.


It may be that more oft than well
 I've woke the melancholy lyre;
Then frown not if I break the spell,
 And touch at times a lighter wire.


If it has been my wont to quaff
 And drain the chalice' darker tide,
What marvel, if I stop and laugh
 To see the satyrs on its side?

## III.

What, though you bid me hoard my hours,
 And say you see my life-star pale,
Have I not walked amid the flowers
 That bloom in the enchanted vale?


Though I had, on a lotus bed,
 Dreamed the wild dreams that few may dare,
Till the o'ershadowing laurel shed
 Its leaves of poison on my hair;

I do believe the gods are just,—
　　They will not break the unfinished chord,
Nor dash the goblet in the dust
　　Until its latest draught be poured.


IV.


Then fill, dear friend, again immerse
　　The lip that shall approve the rhyme;
A richer beauty gilds the verse
　　When seen through cups of Rudesheim.


And if within my tuneful task
　　I wake too oft the mournful note,
Then pour again the golden flask,
　　For it has laughter in its throat.


And while I deem you sit and quaff,
　　I shall no longer be alone,
Nor think my dusty pack and staff
　　My sole companions in Cologne.

# VENICE.

I.

Night on the Adriatic, night!
   And like a mirage of the plain,
With all her marvellous domes of light,
   Pale Venice looms along the main.


No sound from the receding shore,—
   No sound from all the broad lagoon,
Save where the light and springing oar
   Brightens our track beneath the moon :—


Or save where yon high campanile
   Gives to the listening sea its chime;
Or where those dusky giants wheel
   And smite the ringing helm of Time.

'Tis past,—and Venice drops to rest;
　　Alas! hers is a sad repose,
While in her brain and on her breast
　　Tramples the vision of her foes.


Erewhile from her sad dream of pain
　　She rose upon her native flood,
And struggled with the Tyrant's chain,
　　Till every link was stained with blood.


The Austrian pirate, wounded, spurned,
　　Fled howling to the sheltering shore,
But, gathering all his crew, returned
　　And bound the Ocean Queen once more.


'Tis past,—and Venice prostrate lies,—
　　And, snarling round her couch of woes,
The watch-dogs, with the jealous eyes,
　　Scowl where the stranger comes or goes.


## II.

Lo! here awhile suspend the oar;
　　Rest in the Mocenigo's shade,
For Genius hath within this door
　　His charmed, though transient, dwelling made.

Somewhat of " Harold's" spirit yet,
  Methinks, still lights these crumbling halls;
For where the flame of song is set
  It burns, though all the temple falls.


Oh, tell me not those days were given
  To Passion and her pampered brood;
Or that the eagle stoops from heaven
  To dye his talons deep in blood.


I hear alone his deathless strain
  From sacred inspiration won,
As I would only watch again
  The eagle when he nears the sun.

### III.

Oh, would some friend were near me now,
  Some friend well tried and cherished long,
To share the scene;—but chiefly thou,
  Sole source and object of my song.


By Olivola's dome and tower,
  What joy to clasp thy hand in mine,
While through my heart this sacred hour
  Thy voice should melt like mellow wine.

What time or place so fit as this
　　To bid the gondolier withhold,
And dream through one soft age of bliss
　　The olden story, never old?


The domes suspended in the sky
　　Swim all above me broad and fair;
And in the wave their shadows lie,—
　　Twin phantoms of the sea and air.


O'er all the scene a halo plays,
　　Slow fading, but how lovely yet
For here the brightness of past days
　　Still lingers, though the sun is set.


Oft in my bright and boyish hours
　　I lived in dreams what now I live,
And saw these palaces and towers
　　In all the light romance can give.


They rose along my native stream,
　　They charmed the lakelet in the glen;
But in this hour the waking dream
　　More frail and dream-like seems than then.

A matchless scene, a matchless night,
　　A tide below, a moon above;
An hour for music and delight;
　　For gliding gondolas and love!


But here, alas! you hark in vain,—
　　When Venice fell her music died;
And voiceless as a funeral train,
　　The blackened barges swim the tide.


The harp, which Tasso loved to wake,
　　Hangs on the willow where it sleeps,
And while the light strings sigh or break,
　　Pale Venice by the water weeps.

## IV.

'Tis past,—and weary droops the wing
　　That thus hath borne me idly on;
The thoughts I have essayed to sing
　　Are but as bubbles touched and gone.


But Venice, cold his soul must be,
　　Who, looking on thy beauty, hears
The story of thy wrongs, if he
　　Is moved to neither song nor tears.

To glide by temples fair and proud,
　Between deserted marble walls,
Or see the hireling foeman crowd
　Rough-shod her noblest palace halls;


To know her left to Vandal foes
　Until her nest be robbed and gone,—
To see her bleeding breast, which shows
　How dies the Adriatic swan;—


To know that all her wings are shorn;
　That Fate has written her decree,
That soon the nations here shall mourn
　The lone Palmyra of the sea;—


Where waved her vassal flags of yore
　By valour in the Orient won;
To see the Austrian vulture soar,
　A blot against the morning sun;—


To hear a rough and foreign speech
　Commanding the old ocean mart,—
Are mournful sights and sounds that reach,
　And wake to pity, all the heart.

# NIGHTFALL.

### IN MEMORY OF A POET.

I saw in the silent afternoon
  The overladen sun go down;
While, in the opposing sky, the moon,
  Between the steeples of the town,


Went upward, like a golden scale
  Outweighed by that which sank beyond;
And over the river, and over the vale,
  With odours from the lily-pond,


The purple vapours calmly swung;
  And, gathering in the twilight trees,
The many vesper minstrels sung
  Their plaintive mid-day memories,
19

Till, one by one, they dropped away
　　From music into slumber deep;
And now the very woodlands lay
　　Folding their shadowy wings in sleep.


Oh, Peace! that like a vesper psalm
　　Hallows the daylight at its close;
Oh, Sleep! that like the vapour's calm
　　Mantles the spirit in repose,—


Through all the twilight falling dim,
　　Through all the song which passed away,
Ye did not stoop your wings to him
　　Whose shallop on the river lay


Without an oar, without a helm;—
　　His great soul in his marvellous eyes
Gazing on from realm to realm
　　Through all the world of mysteries!

# L'ENVOI.

I BRING the flower you asked of me,
  A simple bloom, nor bright nor rare,
But like a star its light will be
  Within the darkness of your hair.


It grew not in those guarded bowers
  Where rustling fountains sift their spray,
But gladly drank the common showers
  Of dew beside the dusty way.


It may be in its humble sphere
  It cheered the pilgrim of the road,
And shed as blest an alms, as e'er
  The generous hand of Wealth bestowed.

Or though, save mine, it met no eye,
    But secretly looked up and grew,
And from the loving air and sky
    Its little store of beauty drew.


And though it breathed its small perfumes
    So low they did not woo the bee,—
Exalted, how it shines and blooms,
    Above all flowers, since worn by thee.


And thus the song you bade me sing,
    May be a rude and artless lay,
And yet it grew a sacred thing
    To bless me on Life's dusty way.


And unto this, my humble strain,
    How much of beauty shall belong,
If thou wilt in thy memory deign
    To wear my simple flower of song!

# SYLVIA;

## OR,

## THE LAST SHEPHERD.

### AN ECLOGUE.

### AND OTHER POEMS.

**TO**

# Henry C. Townsend, Esq.

To you, my friend, whose youthful feet have known
The same bright hills and valleys as my own;
Whose eye learned beauty from the selfsame scene,
Which, still remembered, keeps our pathways green;
From the same minstrel-stream and poet-birds
Learned what I oft would fain recall in words:—
To you I bring this handful of wild flowers,
By memory plucked from those dear fields of ours;
And when their freshness and their perfume die,
On friendship's shrine still let them fondly lie.

# SYLVIA;

### OR,

## THE LAST SHEPHERD.

# PRELUDE.

---

## THE MERRY MOWERS.

"Here mid the clover's crimson realm
    We'll rest us through the glowing noon,
Beneath this broad and liberal elm,
    Slow nodding to his hundredth June.

"On this low branch our scythes shall sway,
    Fresh reeking from the field in bloom;
While, breathing o'er the new-mown hay,
    The air shall fan us with perfume.

"And here the cottage maid shall spread
  The viands on the stainless cloth,—
The golden prints, the snow-white bread,
  The chilly pitcher crowned with froth.

"And you, fair youth, whose shepherd look
  Brings visions of the pastoral time,—
Your hay-fork shouldered like a crook,
  Your speech the natural voice of rhyme,—

"Although the world is far too ripe
  To hark,—or, hearkening, would disdain,—
Come, pour along your fancied pipe
  The music of some rustic strain.

"We'll listen as we list the birds,—
  And, being pleased, will hold it wise;
And deem we sit mid flocks and herds
  Beneath the far Arcadian skies."

Thus spake the mowers; while the maid,
  The fairest daughter of the realm,
Stood twining in the happy shade
  A wreath of mingled oak and elm.


And this, with acorns interwound,
  And violets inlaid with care,
Fame's temporary priestess bound
  In freshness round her druids hair.


The breeze with sudden pleasure played,
  And, dancing in from bough to bough,
Let one slant sunbeam down, which stayed
  A moment on the crownéd brow.


The birds, as with a newborn thrill,
  Sang as they only sing at morn,
While through the noon from hill to hill
  Echoed the winding harvest-horn.

With upturned face and lips apart,

He mused a little, but not long;

For clustered in his boundless heart

Sang all the morning-stars of song.

# THE ECLOGUE.

## I.

In middle of a noble space,
  Of antique wood and boundless  plain,
Queen Sylvia, regent of all grace,
  Held long-descended reign.

The diadem her forehead wore
  Was her bright hair, a golden band;
And she, as sceptre, ever bore
  A distaff in her hand.

In russet train, with rustling tread,
She walked like morning, dewy-eyed,
And like Saint Agnes, ever led
A white lamb at her side.


And she to all the flowery land
Was dear as are the summer skies;
And round her waving mulberry-wand
Swarmed all the butterflies.


Queen was she of the flaxen skein,
And empress of the snowy fleece,
And o'er the silkworm's small domain
Held guard in days of peace.

## II.

To own her sway the woods were proud,
  The solemn forest, wreathed and old;
To her the pluméd harvests bowed
  Their rustling ranks of gold.

Mantled in majesty complete,
  She walked among her flocks and herds;
Where'er she moved, with voices sweet,
  Sang all her laureate birds.
20

All happy sounds waved softly near,

 With perfume from the fields of dew;

From every hill, bold chanticleer

 His silver clarion blew.


The bees her honey-harvest reaped,

 The fields were murmurous with their glee;

And loyal to her hives, they heaped

 Her waxen treasury.


All pleasures round her loved to press,

 To sing their sweetest madrigals;—

She never knew the weariness

 Which dwells in grander halls.

## III.

What time came in the welcome spring,
   The happy maiden looked abroad,
And saw her lover gayly fling
   The flax athwart the sod.

Hither and thither the yellow seed
   Young Leon sprinkled o'er the plain,
As a farmer to his feathery breed
   Full hands of golden grain.

As o'er the yielding mould he swayed,
He whistled to his measured tread
A happy tune; for he saw the maid
Spinning the future thread.


Or saw the shuttle in her room
Fly, like a bird, from hand to hand;
And then his arm, as at a loom,
Swung wider o'er the land.


He wondered what the woof would be,—
Or for the poor, or for the proud?
A bridal garment fluttering free?
Or formal winding-shroud?

## IV.

THEN May recrossed the southern hill,—
　　Her heralds thronged the elms and eaves;
And Nature, with a sudden thrill,
　　Burst all her buds to leaves.


Loud o'er the slope a streamlet flung
　　Fresh music from its mountain springs,
As if a thousand birds there sung
　　And flashed their azure wings.

"Flow on," the maiden sang, "and whirl,
    Sweet stream, your music o'er the hill,
And touch with your light foot of pearl
    The wheel of yonder mill."


It touched the wheel, and in the vale
    Died from the ear and passed from view,—
Like a singing bird that is seen to sail
    Into the distant blue;—


Died where the river shone below,
    Where white sails through the vapour glowed,
Like great archangels moving slow
    On some celestial road.

## V.

How sweet it is when twilight wakes
    A many-voicéd eve in May,—
When Sylvia's western casement takes
    The farewell flame of day:

When cattle from the upland lead
    Or drive their lengthening shadows home;
While bringing from the odorous mead
    Deep pails of snowy foam.

The milkmaid sings, and, while she stoops,
   Her hands keep time; the night-hawk's wail
Pierces the twilight, till he swoops
   And mocks the sounding pail.


Then sings the robin, he who wears
   A sunset memory on his breast,
Pouring his vesper hymns and prayers
   To the red shrine of the west.


Deep in the grove the woodland sprites
   Start into frequent music brief;
And there the whip-poor-will recites
   The ballad of his grief.


The ploughs turn home; the anvils cease;
   The forge has faded with the sun;
The heart of the loom is soothed to peace,
   And the toiling day is done.

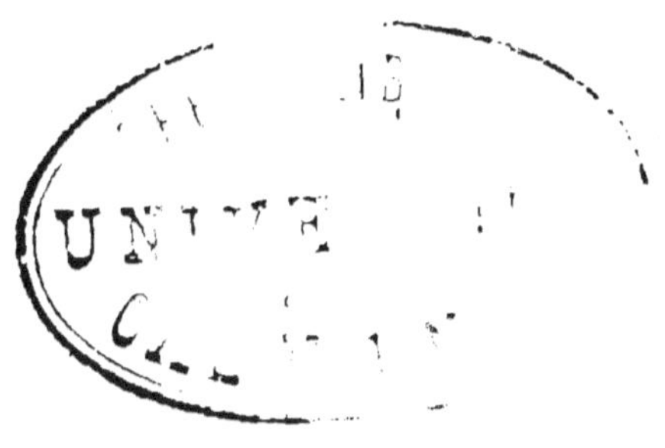

## VI.

A LOVER's heart hath no repose;
'Tis ever thundering in his ear
The story of his joys and woes,—
The light remote, the shadow near.

And Leon, penning his fleecy stock,
.Felt hope as painful as despair,
While one by one heaven's starry flock
Came up the fields of air.

True shepherd,—like the men of old,—
He knew to call each as it came;
And, as his flock leaped in the fold,
Each had a starry name.


There, clustered close in slumbrous peace,
He gazed on them with shepherd pride,
And saw each deep and pillowy fleece
Through Sylvia's soft hands glide.


In that still hour, where none might mark,
He leaned against the shadowy bars;
Soft tearlight blurred the deepening dark
And doubled all the stars.


And, starlike, through the valley dim
The tapers shot their guiding rays;
But one there was which seemed to him
To set the night ablaze.

To his impatient feet it flowed,

    A stream of gold along the sod;

Then like the road to glory glowed

    The love-lit path he trod!

## VII.


Out of her tent, as one afraid,
　　The moon along the purple field
Stole like an oriental maid,
　　　Her beauty half concealed.


And, peering with her vestal torch
　　Between the vines at Sylvia's door,
She saw two shadows in the porch
　　Pass and repass the floor.

On the far hill the dreary hound
    Saddened the evening with his howl;
In the near grove—a shuddering sound—
    Echoed the ominous owl.


Three times, as at a robber band,
    The guardian mastiff leaped his chain;
Three times the hand in Leon's hand
    Grew chill and shook with pain.


And Sylvia said, "These, Leon, these
    Are the dismal sounds which three nights past
Came herald to the mysteries
    Of dreams too sad to last.

## VIII.


"First of the mournful sights, I saw
Our flocks fly bleating from a hound,
And many a one his savage jaw
Dragged bleeding to the ground.


"The rest sought shelter in despair,
And in a brake were robbed and torn;
The cruel hound had an ally there
In every brier and thorn.

"In nightmare chains my feet were set,

    For I could neither move nor scream :—

Oh, Leon, it makes me tremble yet,

    Although 'twas but a dream !


"Anon I struggled forth, and took

    From off our mastiff's neck the chain;

He leaped the gate, he leaped the brook,

    And snarled across the plain.


"Then how they fought !  My sight grew dim,

    In straining to the field remote :

At length he threw that bloodhound grim,

    And held him by the throat !

IX.


"And then I heard your neighing train,—
   Its silver bells rang down the breeze,—
And saw the white arch of your wain
   Between the roadside trees.


"Announced as by an ocean storm,
   A horseman from the east in ire
Rode to retrieve his hound: his form
   Was robed in scarlet fire.

"But when you saw our murdered field—
     And saw in midst the struggling hounds—
And him whose sword made threat to wield
     Destruction o'er our grounds;—


"You loosed the best steed of your team,
     And seized the weapon nearest hand,—
Then sped the hill and leaped the stream,
     And bade the invader stand.


"Then came the horrid sight and sound:
     At length I saw the foe retreat,
And swooned for joy; but waking found
     You bleeding at my feet!

21

## X.


"I bore you in; with my own hand
     I tended you long nights and days;
And heard with pride how all the land
     Was ringing with your praise.


But when your deepest wounds were well,—
     This, Leon, is the saddest part,—
A lady came with witching spell,
     And claimed you, hand and heart.

"She came in all her southern pride;

And, though she was as morning bright,

An Afric bondmaid at her side

Stooped like a starless night.


"She moved as she were monarch born,

And smiled her sweetest smile on you;

But scorned me with her lofty scorn,

Until I shrank from view.


"When you were gone, all hope had flown,—

Grief held to me her bitter crust;

My distaff droped, my loom o'erthrown

Lay trampled in the dust.

## XI.

"I KNOW such dreams are empty, vain;
And yet may rest upon the heart,
Like chillness of a summer rain
After the clouds depart.


"And still the dream went on:—each hour
Some new-born wonder filled the dream:—
First came the labourers to o'erpower
And chain our little stream.

"A giant prison-wall they made;—
Our brook, recoiling in her fears,
Over our meadows wildly strayed,
And drowned them with her tears.

"And then they reared a stately home,—
Not one, but many, for this queen;
The gleam of tower and spire and dome
Through all the land was seen.

"And when her orgies swelled the breeze,
Loudly a mile away or more
Was borne the voice of her revelries,
The rattle and the roar.

XII.

"You grew to her more fond and near,
And mine no more!  Ah, never more
You brought the antlered forest deer
And laid it at my door.


"And ever round the hall and hearth,
These branching emblems of the chase
Mocked me with memory of the mirth
Which once made bright the place.

"No more 'neath autumn's sun or cloud
  You paid to me the pleasing tax
Of labour at the swingle loud,
  Breaking the brittle flax.

"No more when winter walked our clime
  We woke the evening-lighted room,
With laugh and song, still keeping time
  To whirring wheel or loom.

"Nor blazed the great logs as of yore,
  Cheered with the cricket's pastoral song;
The cider and the nuts were o'er,
  And gone the jovial throng

"The hearth was basely narrowed down;
  The antlered walls were stripped and bare;
The oaken floor no more was known,—
  A foreign woof was there.

## XIII.


"And never more your ringing team
    Made music in our happy dale;
Instead, an earthquake winged with steam
    Roared through our sundered vale.


"And where yon river seaward runs,
    The white-winged barges ceased to roam;
Instead, came great leviathans
    Trampling the waves to foam.

"And there was rushing to and fro,
  As if the nation suddenly
Made haste to meet some foreign foe
  Impending on the sea.


"And all this horrid roar and rage—
  The clash of steel and flash of ire
Was the giant march of the Conquering Age
  Flapping his flags of fire!


"He strode the land from east to west:—
  Then death in my despair was sweet,
And soon above my buried breast
  Trampled the world's loud feet.


"The dreary dream is past and told;
  But, Leon, swear to still be true,
Even though with charms a thousandfold
  A queen should smile on you."

This, Leon swore,—swore still to pay

The fealty he long had borne;

The years which followed best can say

If Leon was forsworn.

## XIV.

"Forsworn!" The fields all sighed, "forsworn!"
When Sylvia pined into her shroud;
And all the pastures lay forlorn,
O'ershadowed with a cloud.

The homesteads wept with childish sob,
"Forsworn!" and every wheel was dumb;
The looms were muffled, each low throb
Was like a funeral drum.

The maidens hid in Maytime grots,
　　Their distaffs twined with blossoms sweet,
With pansies and forget-me-nots,
　　And laid them at her feet.


"Forsworn!" they sighed, and sprinkled o'er
　　Her breast the loveliest flowers of May;
And then these fair pall-bearers bore
　　Her gentle dust away.


"Forsworn!"　The grandams moved about
　　Like useless shadows in their gloom;
And oft they brought their distaffs out,
　　And sat beside her tomb.


"Forsworn!"　All nature sighs, "forsworn!"
　　And Sylvia's is a nameless grave;
The blossoms which above her mourn
　　Mid tangled grasses wave.

## XV.

PROUD Leon sits beside his bride,
   His chariot manned by Nubian grooms,—
His lady rustling in the pride
   Of stuffs of foreign looms.

Secure, important, and serene,
   The master of a wide domain,
He looks abroad with lordly mien,—
   This once poor shepherd swain.

You scarce would think to see him now,
In all his grandeur puffed and full,
He e'er had guided flock or plough
In simple, homespun wool.


The chain of gold is still a chain;—
There may be moments he would pay
The bulk of all his marvelous gain
For what has passed away!

# CONCLUSION.

---

## THE MOURNFUL MOWERS.

Thus sang the shepherd crowned at noon,
  And every breast was heaved with sighs;—
Attracted by the tree and tune,
  The wingéd singers left the skies.

Close to the minstrel sat the maid;
  His song had drawn her fondly near:
Her large and dewy eyes betrayed
  The secret to her bosom dear.

The factory people through the fields,
  Pale men and maids and children pale,
Listened, forgetful of the wheels,
  Till the loud summons woke the vale.


And all the mowers rising said,
  "The world has lost its dewy prime;
Alas! the Golden age is dead,
  And we are of the Iron time!


"The wheel and loom have left our homes,—
  Our maidens sit with empty hands,
Or toil beneath yon roaring domes,
  And fill the factory's pallid bands.


"The fields are swept as by a war,
  Our harvests are no longer blithe;
Yonder the iron mower's car
  Comes with his devastating scythe.

"They lay us waste by fire and steel,
   Besiege us to our very doors;
Our crops before the driving wheel
   Fall captive to the conquerors.

"The pastoral age is dead, is dead!
   Of all the happy ages chief;
Let every mower bow his head,
   In token of sincerest grief.

"And let our brows be thickly bound
   With every saddest flower that blows;
And all our scythes be deeply wound
   With every mournful leaf that grows."

Thus sang the mowers; and they said,
   "The world has lost its dewy prime;
Alas! the Golden age is dead,
   And we are of the Iron time!"

22

Each wreathed his scythe and twined his head;
   They took their slow way through the plain:
The minstrel and the maiden led
   Across the fields the solemn train.


The air was rife with clamorous sounds,
   Of clattering factory—thundering forge,—
Conveyed from the remotest bounds
   Of smoky plain and mountain gorge.


Here, with a sudden shriek and roar,
   The rattling engine thundered by;
A steamer past the neighbouring shore
   Convulsed the river and the sky.


The brook that erewhile laughed abroad,
   And o'er one light wheel loved to play,
Now, like a felon, groaning trod
   Its hundred treadmills night and day.

The fields were tilled with steeds of steam,
  Whose fearful neighing shook the vales;
Along the road there rang no team,—
  The barns were loud, but not with flails.


And still the mournful mowers said,
  "The world has lost its dewy prime;
Alas! the Golden age is dead,
  And we are of the Iron time!"

# Miscellaneous.

# THE BLESSED DEAD.

Oh, happy childhood! tender buds of spring

  Touched in the Maytime by a wandering frost;

Ye have escaped the summer's sultry wing:

  No drought hath parched you, and no wind hath tossed,

Shaking the pearls of morning from your breast:

  Ye have been gathered ere your sweets were lost,

Ere wingéd passions stole into your rest

  To rob the heart of all its dewy store.

Now in the endless Maytime overhead,

  In starry gardens of the azure shore,

  Ye bloom in light, and are for evermore

    The blessed dead.

Ye youths and maidens, dear to Joy and Love,
  But fallen midway between morn and noon,—
Or bird-like flown, as if some longing dove
  Should seek a better clime while yet 'tis June,
Leaving our fields forlorn!  Oh, happy flight!
  Gone while your hearts are full of summer tune
And ignorant of the autumnal blight,—
  Ere yet a leaf hath withered on the bough
Or innocent rose hath drooped its dying head:
  Gone with the virgin lilies on your brow,
    Ye, singing in immortal youth, are now
      The blessed dead.

And ye, who in the harvest of your years
  Were stricken when the sun was in mid air,
And left the earth bedewed at noon with tears,—
  Ye have known all of life that is most fair,
The laugh of April and the summer bloom.
  Ye with the orange-blossoms in your hair,
Who sleep in bridal chambers of the tomb;

Or ye, who with the sickle in the hand
Have bowed amid the sheaves the manly head,
And left the toil unto a mournful band,—
Ye all are numbered in yon resting land,
The blessed dead.


And ye, who like the stately upland oak
Breasted the full allotted storms of time,
And took new strength from every gusty stroke,—
And ye, who like a vine long taught to climb
And weigh its native branches with ripe fruit,—
Much have ye suffered 'neath the frosty rime
Which autumn brings and winter's loud dispute!
But now, transplanted in the fields afar,
Your age is like a withered foliage shed,—
And where Youth's fountain sparkles like a star,
This have ye learned, they only live who are
The blessed dead.

# THE PHANTOM LEADERS.

By starlight they rode in their speed and their might,

A warrior host sweeping down through the night,—

An army of spectres, they sped on the wind,

With swords piercing front and plumes streaming
behind;

On the highways of air they were led as by Mars,

While their steeds shod with thunder seemed trampling the stars!

Like a fleet in a gale, they careered through the
night,

And the path where they passed flashed with phos-
phorous light.

In the front galloped Brutus, a foe to all peace,

His blade gleaming red with the blood of Lucrece;

And, turning towards Rome, bent his way down the

heaven,

Repeating the oath which of old he had given.

"These modern Tarquins must fall!" was his cry;

"By the blade of their own bloody guilt they shall

die!"

And, strange though it be, there Mohammed was seen,

His Arab's mane sweeping his mantle of green,

And the watchwords engraved on his drawn scimetar

Were "Allah, il Allah!" each letter a star.

Gustavus-Adolphus of Sweden was there,

As at Lützen he rode with his battle-blade bare.

And, like their own turbulent torrents let loose

By a storm in the Highlands, sped Wallace and Bruce.

Sobieski, the Pole, gave his charger the rein,

Every stroke of whose hoof broke a fetter in twain.

There was Olaf of Norway, whose mandate and sword

The heathen struck down in the name of the Lord.

There sped fiery Tell with his crossbow and dart,
The barb glowing crimson from Gessler's proud heart.
And close by his side, the beloved of his peers,
Bold Winklereid rode with his arms full of spears;
The same old self-sacrifice lighting his eye,
And "Make way for Liberty!" still was his cry.
There was Luther, no braver e'er rode to the field,
And the word of the Lord was his buckler and shield,
While the weapon he grasped was the same he had
    sped
In a moment of anger at Lucifer's head.
There was Cromwell, that monarch who never wore
    crown,
With his Bible and sword and his puritan frown
And with him Charles-Albert, the Piedmontese star,
As he rode ere betrayed on the field of Novarre.
There with garments still red from that last fatal day,
The ghost of Bozzaris sped fierce for the fray;
And close by his side, with an eye full of fire,
Rode Byron, still grasping his sword and his lyre:

And the war-kindling numbers which fell from his
    tongue
Like the notes of a wild battle-clarion were flung!
And just in advance galloped Körner and Burns
Unsheathing the war-song and falchion by turns!
There, gazing and listening, my spirit entranced
Leaped for joy as these poets for Freedom advanced;
And I felt the warm thought through my bosom
    descend,
That the bard to be true must be Liberty's friend!

Then came a dim host to my vision unknown,
Like those lights which astronomers number alone;
But their voice still made clear what the eye could
    not see,
Crying, "Down with the tyrant wherever he be!"

But why swept these phantoms? Whence rode they,
    and where?
What occasion had summoned these allies of air?

I looked, and beheld the swift spread of the blaze

Which dazzled the stars with the pulse of its rays,

As if through the darkness the lightning had played,

And in midst of its splendour been suddenly stayed:

There I read the great words spread like fiery wings

Where "weighed and found wanting" confronted the

kings!

And this army of spectres, led on by that light,

Like a cloud on a hurricane swept through the night;

And this was their cry coming down on the gale,

"The modern Belshazzars are weighed in the scale!"

# A BIRTHDAY THOUGHT IN ITALY.

INSCRIBED TO MISS S. R. B.

As once the trembling Lombard saw
  The swift barbarians' line of spears
Wind down the Alps, thus here in awe
  I watch the approaching line of years.

They come, the Goth and vandal bands,
  With savage tread and look uncouth;
With spear and mace and murderous brands,
  They file towards the plains of youth.

Down into life's Etrurian vales,
  O'er green campagnas broad and fair,
They sweep like bitter Nor'land gales,
  And fright the calm Italian air.


Their barbarous feet know no restraint;
  They vent their rage before our eyes:
The shrines that held our dearest saint
  A ruined heap before us lies.


The temples by our young hearts reared,
  Their ruffian malice batters down;
Ambition's altars, unrevered,
  With domes of Hope, lie overthrown.


And Friendship's wayside shrines and towers
  Too oft are shattered as they pass:
Oft Love, a statue wreathed with flowers,
  Lies at their feet a crumbled mass.

But like these pure Etruscan skies,

Unsullied by the Goth's control,

One fane the vandal Time defies,—

The dome of sunshine in the soul!


And thou, fair maid, so young and blest!

When impious years shall touch thy brow,

Still hold this sunshine in thy breast,

And be as beautiful as now.


*Bagna di Lucca*, August 16, 1855.

# THE STAYED CURSE.

With face half hidden in ungathered hair,
Which fell like sunshine o'er her shoulders bare,
She leaned her cheek against her chamber wall,
As if to note when some far voice should call.
Her weary soul stood at its prison bars,
Fainting to hear a summons from the stars:
For life was now a midnight wilderness,
Wherein none whispered peace to her distress,
Save One, whose voice, of love and pity blended,
Mid her loud grief was not yet comprehended.

She heard alone the vulture sailing by,

Led by the foulest birds of calumny;

Felt the cold serpents crawl against her feet,

And saw the gaunt wolves steal to her retreat.

The wide world scowled and reddened at her shame,

Scorching her soul with horror; and her name

Was struck, as with the violent hand of rage,

With one huge blot from off the social page.

What wonder that the soul thus rudely wrung

Should shape such words as half appalled the tongue!

Words like fierce arrows for the faithless breast

Where love had dreamed with too confiding rest;

Shafts which, once sped at random from the lips,

Some friendly fiend must guide to their eclipse

In the dark heart, where, on his starless throne,

Deception sat, and, smiling, reigned alone!


Thus had she nursed her grief for many days,

　　And thus the curse was struggling from her breast,

When, as the midnight's solemn sentry bell
Struck vaguely through her woe-engendered haze,
  Announcing, as it were, the mournful guest,
  She heard the sudden close of wings which fell,
Together with the rustling sound of sighs;
And presently, uplifting her blank eyes,
  Beheld a dull and ashen form of woe
    Stand looking its great melancholy there,
    As if long years of under-world despair
Had fanned him with the hottest airs that blow
Athwart the fierce Sahara fields below!
The wings were leaden-hued and ruffled all,
As if long beaten 'gainst some stormy wall,
Or blown contrary by belligerent gusts,
Then trailed for ages through the cinder dusts
On plains adjacent, where the Stygian pours,
Hissing forever on volcanic shores!
She looked, and on her lips the curse was stayed!
  Thrice all the vengeance which her soul had planned

Burned on the forehead of the fallen shade!

 Her purpose dropt—as from the archer's hand
Might fall the arrow if he saw the foe
Struck by the lightning's swift and surer blow!
The curse was stayed—she looked to heaven and sighed,
"Forgive! forgive!" and in her prayer she died!

# TWENTY-ONE.



FAR within the orient azure,
   In the purple and the dew,
Lies the flowery land of pleasure
   Which your early childhood knew.

In its dim and blue existence
   There it lies, a dewy space,
In the bright forbidden distance
   Memory only can retrace.

After this the fancy wanders
  Over varied field and hill,
Where the swelling stream meanders
  And forgets it was a rill.


Many a flower with odours baneful
  Blooms enticingly thereby,
To whose influence, subtle, painful,
  Later years shall testify.


In Youth's lovely, dangerous valley,
  E'en the best directed feet
Oft may turn to stray and dally
  Mid the bowers that chill and cheat.


But anon the flowers grow scanter
  And to rougher pastures yield,
Where the ploughman and the planter
  Must prepare the harvest-field.

On that boundary you are standing,
  'Twixt the blossoms and the clods,
To begin on this stern landing
  The great strife 'gainst fearful odds.

Where you strolled the sunny meadows,
  You must brave the rocks and storms;
Where you took alarm at shadows,
  You must combat solid forms.

Hills of snow and valleys torrid
  Lie beyond the boundary vast,
Where fond Life with anxious forehead
  Reads the future from the past.

Huge and rough as thunder-smitten,
  Rise the barriers of the gate,
With one sentence overwritten,—
  Simple letters full of fate.

On the arch through which you're speeding
　　There those two forbidding words
Still shall flame, as over Eden
　　Blazed the red exiling swords.


A lost realm recovered never—
　　With receding speed increased,
Barred and branded there forever
　　It shall glimmer in the east.


Youth is gone—a vanished glory—
　　And, with stern and earnest view,
Manhood needs take up the story,
　　And with valour bear it through.


All the world lies wide before you,
　　Where to choose the wrong or right;
And no future shall restore you
　　What you seize not now with might.

Let each act be the sure token

    Of the nobler life ahead :—

Let each thought in truth be spoken,

    Though the utterance strike you dead.


Spurn the small enticing by-way

    Where Temptation sits apart :

Boldly tread the open highway

    Leading to the golden mart.


Though the world smile on you blandly,

    Let your friends be choice and few :

Choose your course, pursue it grandly,

    And achieve what you pursue !

# BEATRICE.

Though others know thee by a fonder name,
  I, in my heart, have christened thee anew;
  And though thy beauty, in its native hue,
(Shedding the radiance of whence it came,)
May not bequeath to language its high claim,—
  Thy smiling presence, like an angel's wing,
Fans all my soul of poesy to flame,—
  Till, even in remembering, I must sing.
Such led the grand old Tuscan's longing eyes
Through all the crystal rounds of Paradise;
  And, in my spirit's farthest journeying,
Thy smile of courage leads me up the skies,
Through realms of song, of beauty, and of bliss,—
And therefore have I named thee Beatrice!

# HERO AND LEANDER.

Long had they dwelt within one breathless cell,
   Two souls, by some mad Sycorax confined;
But, oh! the unmeant mercy of that spell
   Which turned those arms to marble, while entwined
In all the passionate wo of tenderness,
   And to the unknown depths of earth consigned,—
These radiant forms of Beauty's rare excess,
This monument of Love's own loveliness!

Unchronicled, the centuries rolled on,
   And groves grew ancient on the prison-hill;

And men forgot their parent tongues anon,

  And spoke a different language, as a rill

Wearing another channel from its source,

Makes a new song accordant with its course.

But suddenly the unexpectant sun

  Beheld the swarthy labourers employ

Upon that hill their rude exhuming art,

Like shadowy hopes at some dull, ancient heart,

  To free the spirit of long buried joy.

And now they grappled with the stubborn rocks,

  Breaking the antique seals which time had set

Upon the earth's deep treasury, that locks

  Within its inmost wards such marts as yet

The busy masons of the poet's brain

  Have builded not.  Anon the toiling ox

Dragged the white quarry to the peopled plain,

  And Beauty's soul lay sepulchred unknown!

The crowd discerned it not, till there came one

Who heard the passionate breathings in the stone,

The wordless music of Love's overflow;

Who heard and pitied, and, like Prospero,

   Released the spirits from their living grave;

And when the breathless world beheld them—lo!

The soul of purity, around, above,

Hung in the tremulous air like heaven's own dove;

   And Fame pronounced the name of him who gave

A marble immortality to Love!

# WINTER.

Lo, Winter comes, and all his heralds blow
Their gusty trumpets, and his tents of snow
Usurp the fields from whence sad Autumn flies,—
Autumn, that finds a southern clime or dies.
The streams are dumb with wo,—the forest grieves,
Wailing the loss of all its summer leaves:
As some fond Rachel on her childless breast
Clasps her thin hands where once her young were prest;
Then flings her empty arms into the air,
And swells the gale with her convulsed despair!

# THE BLIGHTED FLOWER.

Why, gentle lady, why complain
　　At Scandal's ever flying breath?
'Gainst Virtue's cheek it blows in vain,
　　And thereon breathes itself to death.

The flower beneath the passing rain,
　　Untouched of canker or of blight,
Bows patiently, to rise again
　　With sweeter breath and fresher light.

But if the worm be hid beneath,
　Or haply if the hot simoom,
Like some unlawful lover's breath,
　Hath wooed that blossom to its doom,—

Then, wo is me, how poor and frail
　Is Beauty in her fairest form!
Her brightness cannot stay the gale,
　Her perfume cannot charm the storm.

But when the searching wind comes by,
　And shakes each blossom by the stalk,
The tainted leaves asunder fly,
　To wither down the garden walk;—

And ere one heated noon has sped,
　They crisp and curl and pass from sight;
Or crumble 'neath some careless tread
　As if they never had been bright.
24

# THE DEATH OF THE VETERAN.

## AN INCIDENT DURING THE MEXICAN WAR.

### Inscribed

### TO MAJOR ANDERSON OF THE U. S. ARMY.

SINCE last we met, a throng has joined
  The army of the years,
Trampling to dust our summer flowers,
  Like conquering cavaliers.
Since last we met! — In those few words
  There is a mournful beat,
Like throbbing of a muffled drum,
  Or tread of funeral feet.
Since then, in war's high festival,
  You've waved the clashing sword, —
While I have been a saddened guest
  At Life's promiscuous board.
Since then, the young with mimic arms
  Have grown to arméd men;

And they may wear the veteran's hair
    Before we meet again : —
Or though, ere that, our mighty Chief
    Should grant our last release,
And Death conduct us to the camp,
    The far white camp of Peace, —
Yet here, in memory of those days,
    Still cherished, though long spent,
I wake the martial harp before
    The doorway of your tent.

---

FROM hill to hill the "good news" ran
  As swift as signal fires;
From shore to sea, from gulf to land,
  And flashed along the wires:

And presently from wharf to wharf
  The cannons made reply,
And in the city's crowded streets
  Was heard the newsman's cry.

Bright grew the matron's face when I
   The victory began;
Pale waxed the young wife's cheek when she
   Heard who had led the van;

And struggling with the mists of age
   Which veiled his eye and ear,
The grandsire raised his palsied hand
   And feebly strove to hear.

And when I read the story, how
   Amid the flying balls
The brave lieutenant bore the flag
   And scaled the shattered walls;

The matron and the young wife stood
   Too terrified for tears,
While flamed the old man's cheek with red
   It had not known for years.

But when I read, that as the flag
  In triumph o'er him flew,
How twenty bullets hewed his breast
  And cleaved it through and through,—

The mother heaved a short, deep groan,
  And sunk into her chair;
The wife fell on the matron's breast,
  And swooned in her despair.

And like a wounded, dying stag,
  Lodged in some old retreat,
That hears the still approaching hounds
  And staggers to his feet,—

The Veteran struggled from his chair
  And raised himself upright,—
His eye a moment kindled with
  Its long forgotten light;—

So firm he strode across the room,
  So martial was his air,
You scarce had guessed that ninety years
  Had whitened through his hair:—


Then from the wainscot took his sword
  Where it had hung so long,
Memorial of many a field,
  The weak against the strong,—


Of fields where Justice armed the few
  With consecrated brands,
And lodged a nation's destiny
  In their devoted hands:—


And, gazing on the blade, he said,
  "Thou art as keen and bright
As when in those old trying times
  We battled for the right;

As when we wintered in the snow
   Within the frozen gorge,
And from our starving ranks still hurled
   Defiance at King George :—


As when beside the Brandywine
   We fought the whole day through,
Till fields had changed their mantle
   And the river changed its hue :—


As when mid grinding gulfs of ice,
   Upon a Christmas night,
We crossed the roaring Delaware
   And put the foe to flight !


It may be this old arm of mine
   Is not as steady now
As when it drew against Burgoyne,
   Or cleaved the ranks of Howe ;

The hand may tremble on the hilt,
　The heart within is strong;
And God who strengthened once the right
　Will not uphold the wrong.

What! have they ta'en the last support
　That propped my honoured wall?
Shall the name become tradition
　And the stately roof-tree fall?

Was't not enough that he who, through
　The woods and tangled brakes,
Spread terror o'er the savage, from
　The Gulf unto the lakes;

And who beside the bloody Thames
　Left death where'er he sped,
Till the fate which he was hurling round
　Recoiled upon his head?

Was't not enough?  Speak thou, my friend:
  Old comrade, thou wert there,
Who in the days aforetime drove
  The Lion to his lair;

Twice drove him from our shore, and chased
  The red wolf to his den!
Wast't not enough, but must I hear
  The death-note sound again?

And has our banner waved abroad,
  The martial trumpet pealed,
And foemen bristled on the plain,
  And we not in the field?

Old sword, in this our winter,
  Shall they call to us in vain,
Who reaped the crimson harvest
  With a Washington and Wayne?

No! come, my trusty champion,
  Till the field be cleared and won,
And the foe be left in prostrate ranks
  To bleach beneath the sun!

Ho! now is't blood which stains you,
  Or the shameful blush of rust?
Is it age which dims my vision,
  Or the flying smoke and dust?

Is't the beating of my heart I hear,
  Or calling drum at hand?
Or grows my steps unsteady,
  Or does battle shake the land?

The drums grow loud and louder,
  With the bugle's dreadful note:
The smoke-wreaths thicken round me,
  And the dust is in my throat!

Hark, hark!  I hear the order, and
  It bids me mount the wall;
I know the General's voice!—and I
  Obey him though I fall!


Yes, I will plant my country's flag
  Upon the topmost stone;
For when her fate demands it,
  What should I care for my own?


Now how the loud walls totter,—
  Thicker,—darker grows the smoke,—
And all the air is turned to dust,—
  I stumble, and I choke!


One solid thrust to plant the staff,—
  There!—let the eagle soar!"
He cried, and reeling, clasped his breast,—
  He fell—and breathed no more!

# EVENING IN WINTER.

Robed like an abbess
The snowy earth lies,
While the red sundown
Fades out of the skies.
Up walks the evening
Veiled like a nun,
Telling her starry beads
One by one.

Where like the billows
The shadowy hills lie,

Like a mast the great pine swings
  Against the bright sky.
Down in the valley
  The distant lights quiver,
Gilding the hard-frozen
  Face of the river.

When o'er the hilltops
  The moon pours her ray,
Like shadows the skaters
  Skirr wildly away;
Whirling and gliding,
  Like summer-clouds fleet,
They flash the white lightning
  From glittering feet.

The icicles hang
  On the front of the falls,
Like mute horns of silver
  On shadowy walls;

Horns that the wild huntsman
Spring shall awake,
Down flinging the loud blast
Toward river and lake!

# A PLEA FOR THE HOMELESS.

A CRY goes up amidst a prosperous nation,
    And Hunger begs within a plenteous land!
Have ye not heard the voice of Desolation?
    Have ye not seen the stretched and famished hand?
Have ye not felt the solemn obligation
    To rise, and straightway answer the demand?


O happy mothers, in your homes protected,
    Whose little ones may never ask for alms,
That voice is Childhood's! starving and neglected,
    Pale Infancy implores with empty palms,—
The sad soul sitting in its eyes dejected,
    No voice elates, no smile of pity calms.

Let those dear looks, so full of April splendour,
  Those dimpled hands you clasp within your own,
That voice you love so, plead with accents tender,
  For those who weep unguarded and alone,
For those dull eyes, those hands so weak and slender,
  Those pallid lips, whose mirth is but a moan!


Sweet plants there are which bloom in sultry places,
  By rude feet trampled in their early hour,
Which, when transplanted, are so full of graces,
  They lend a charm to Flora's fairest bower;
O ye who pass, look down into their faces,
  Displace the dust, and recognise the flower!


Lo, the example for our guidance given,—
  In sacred light our duty stands revealed!
For ONE there was, who, in His great love, even
  Noted the smallest lilies of the field,—
And blessing children, said, "Of such is heaven!"
  His "suffer them to come," stands unrepealed!

O ye whose hearts, amid the worldly noises,
  No cares can harden, and no self benumb,
Whose ears are open to these orphan voices,
  Whose answering soul no avarice makes dumb,
The great RECORDER o'er your names rejoices,
  For ye have truly suffered them to come !
25

# THE CELESTIAL ARMY.

I stood by the open casement
  And looked upon the night,
And saw the westward-going stars
  Pass slowly out of sight.

Slowly the bright procession
  Went down the gleaming arch,
And my soul discerned the music
  Of their long triumphal march;

Till the great celestial army,
  Stretching far beyond the poles,
Became the eternal symbol
  Of the mighty march of souls.


Onward, forever onward,
  Red Mars led down his clan;
And the Moon, like a mailéd maiden,
  Was riding in the van.


And some were bright in beauty,
  And some were faint and small,
But these might be in their great height
  The noblest of them all.


Downward, forever downward,
  Behind Earth's dusky shore
They passed into the unknown night,
  They passed, and were no more.

No more!  Oh, say not so!
   And downward is not just;
For the sight is weak and the sense is dim
   That looks through heated dust.


The stars and the mailéd moon,
   Though they seem to fall and die,
Still sweep with their embattled lines
   An endless reach of sky.


And though the hills of Death
   May hide the bright array,
The marshalled brotherhood of souls
   Still keeps its upward way.


Upward, forever upward,
   I see their march sublime,
And hear the glorious music
   Of the conquerors of Time.

And long let me remember,

   That the palest, fainting one

May to diviner vision be

   A bright and blazing sun.

# Airs from Alpland.

## TO

# Marcus L. Ward, Esq.

To you, who, in the broad commercial plain,
Sittest where calm Passaic seeks the main,
I bring these mountain airs,—and wake once more
The minstrel harp you kindly heard of yore:
Beside your fire the heavenward hill would rear,
And give the pleasures of the mountaineer;
Would wake the music of the marvellous pass,
And loose the avalanche's monster mass;
Recall, had I such mastery o'er the strings,
From St. Bernard the tempest's wildest wings!
Assured the dreariest scene would soon depart
Before your glowing hearth and genial heart!

# THE LISTENERS.

Under the vernal tents of shadowy trees,—
A druid depth of oaken solitude,
The home of wild flowers and the haunt of bees,
The native vale of many a minstrel brood,—
There ran a stream in its bewildering mood
Of song and silence and low whispering trance;
And streamlike paths went winding through the wood
From rock to glen, the temples of Romance,
And there were lawns where Mirth might lead her
wreathéd dance.

Upon a knoll o'ergrown with mosses sweet,

While dropt the sun adown the afternoon,

A group of maidens made their merry seat,—

June all around and in their hearts was June;

And on their flowery lips the mellow tune

Of early summer; and with fingers fair

Shaking the wingéd spoilers in their swoon

From honey-bells of blossoms bright and rare,

They wove their woodland wreaths and decked each

     other's hair.


But when they saw me pass between the trees,

Slow making toward the streamlet's yellow sands,

"Come hither, thou new-comer from the seas,

And sing to us fresh songs of foreign lands!"

They cried, and placed a harp into my hands:

And straightway I went stumbling o'er the strings,

As best I could, to answer their demands,—

Like some poor bird that with his trembling wings

Beats at the caging wires, and to his mistress sings.

# THE FAIR PILGRIM.

"Upon her little palfrey white
Y° maiden sitteth eke upright,—
Her hair is black as y° midnight,
    Her eyes also.
Her cheeks have snary dimples in,
And Cupid's thumb hath touched her chin,
And silken soft her lily skin,—
Her lips like crimson rose-leaves bin
    About her teeth of snow."

TIME was when, with the unrestraint

Of an enamoured soul and hand,—

In lieu of these cold words, that faint

And waver like a willow wand

Before the vision I would paint,—

I would have seized the ready brush,

And, with the limner's clearer art,

Poured out the softer hues that flush
And flow within the painter's heart;
  Have shown you where she passed or stood,
Between the Alpine light and shade;
  Her stately form, her air subdued,
  Her dark eye mellowing to the mood
That round her inmost spirit played.

  I would have wrought the daylight through
To give what yet before me beams,
  And ceased at eve but to renew
The impassioned labour in my dreams.
  But this is past: life takes and gives,
And o'er the dust of hopes long gone
  The vision brightens as it lives,
And mocks the hand that would have drawn.


Along those windings high and vast,
  Through frequent sun and shade she stole,
And all the Alpine splendour passed
  Into the chambers of her soul;

For she was of that better clay
  'Which treads not oft this earthly stage:
Such charméd spirits lose their way
  But once or twice into an age.
Her voice was one that thrills and clings
  Forever in the hearer's bosom,—
As when a bee with flashing wings
  Cleaves to the centre of a blossom,—
And with the mule-bells' measured chime
Her fancies rung themselves to rhyme.

# SONG ON ST. BERNARD.

Oh, it is a pleasure rare
  Ever to be climbing so,
Winding upward through the air,
  Till the cloud is left below!
Upward and forever round
  On the stairway of the stream,
With the motion and the sound
  Of processions in a dream:
While the world below all this
Lies a fathomless abyss.


Freedom singeth ever here,
  Where her sandals print the snow,

And to her the pines are dear,
  Freely rocking to and fro;
Swinging oft like stately ships,
  Where the billowy tempests sport;
Or, as when the anchor slips
  Down the dreamy wave in port,
Standing silent as they list
Where the zephyrs furl the mist.


Here the well-springs drop their pearls,
  All to Freedom's music strung;
And the brooks, like mountain girls,
  Sing the songs of Freedom's tongue.
And the great hills, stern and staunch,
  Guard her valleys and her lakes,
And the rolling avalanche
  Blocks the path the invader makes,
While her eagle, like a flag,
Floats in triumph o'er the crag!
26

# I HAVE LOOKED ON A FACE.

I HAVE looked on a face that has looked in my heart,
  As deep as the moon ever fathoms a wave;
As uncomprehended it came to depart,
  While a sense of its glory was all that it gave.


Where she passed the Alp blossoms grew pallid and
    shrank,
  As a taper in sunlight sinks faint and aghast;
And now o'er her path swims a terrible blank,
  A gulf in the air where her beauty hath passed.

But her light in my heart, which no time can eclipse,

 Seems to brighten and smile in the joy it confers;

And a voice which is shed from aerial lips

 Breathes a music I know which can only be hers!

# THE CHAMOIS HUNTER.

"There!—see you not upon the face
　　Of yonder far and dizzy height
　A something with slow-moving pace,
　　Now faintly seen, now lost to sight?
　And now again, with downward spring,
　As if supported by a wing,
　It drops, then scarcely seems to crawl
　Along the smooth and shining wall.
　Is it a bird? or beast whose lair
　Is hid within some cavern there?

Or some adventurer who hath striven

To scale that Babel wall to heaven?

In sooth, methinks, there never yawned

A passage to the world beyond

Of shorter access than now lies

Around that climber in the skies."


Then spake the guide:—

      " Unless I err,

There is but one adventurer

 From Basle unto Geneva's lake,

From Neufchatel to Splügen pass,

 Of all who freely scale the brow

Of ice that crowns the Mer-de-glace,

 Or climbs the slippery Rosenlau,

 Who dares that dreadful path to take.

Not him who sprang from ridge to ridge,

And passed us on the Devil's Bridge,

And told you all that perilous tale

Which made your rosy cheeks grow pale.

Nor him who in the Grimsel sang

Among his fellows of the chase,

Until the laughing rafters rang

And scared all slumber from the place;

Or, if the weary traveller slept,

Through all his dream the chamois swept

There never yet was hunter born

So fierce of soul, so lithe of limb,

So fearless on the mountain's rim,

As Herman of the Wetterhorn.

He robbed the Jungfrau of her fame,

And put the chamois' flight to shame;

He takes the wild crag by the brow,

As boatman might his shallop-prow.

The avalance he loves to dare,

To shout amid the wild uproar

Until the thundering vale is full,—

Then stands upon the ruins there,

Like some brave Spanish matadore

With foot upon the fallen bull!

"If all goes well as it should go,

Two toiling hours of steady pace

Must bring us to the ribs of snow

That lie around the broken base

Of that far height, and one hour more

Should find us at the convent door;

And there perchance will Herman be,

His shoulder laden with chamois,

His heart a mountain well of glee,

His voice an alpine gust of joy."


Two hours they toiled with steady pace,

And they had gained that rocky base.

But when the winding line had earned

A jutting crag and partly turned,

A sharp and sudden rifle-crack

Broke through the thin and icy air,

Jarring the frozen silence there,

And rattled down the steep hill-side;

But ere the snow-cliffs gave it back,
A wounded chamois in their track
  Rolled bleeding, and there died!
The startled rider checked his rein;
  And the pedestrian stayed his pace:
With looks of wonder or of pain
  Each stared into the other's face.
And when the maid's first shock of fear
  In gentle tremblings passed away,
Her dark eye glistening with a tear,
  She gazed where the dead creature lay.


The graceful head,—the slender horns,—
  The eyes which Death seemed scarce to dull,
  So wildly sad,—so beautiful!
The polished hoofs,—the shining form,—
The limbs that had outsped the storm,
  Thrilled her with wonder and with wo,
Until she would have given a part
Of the dear life-blood of her heart

To wake once more that gentle eye
And bid the eagle's rival fly
   Unto his native crags of snow.


Before their wonder all had passed
A voice came down the rising blast,—
A voice that gayly soared and fell
Along the wild winds' wandering swell;
A carol like a flying bird's—
   Faint were the notes at first, and then
The sounds ran eddying into words
   That sang of mirth and Meyringen.

# SONG OF THE CHAMOIS HUNTER.

Oh, brave may be those bands, perchance,
　Who ride where tropic deserts glow,—
Who bring with lasso and with lance
　The tiger to their saddle's prow :—
But I would climb the snowy track
　Alone, as I have ever been,
And with a chamois on my back,
　Descend to merry Meyringen.


Oh, they may sing of eyes of jet,
　That melt in passion's dreamy glance,—

Of forms that to the castanet

   Sway through the languor of the dance :—

But let me clasp some blue-eyed girl,

   Whose arms impulsive clasp again;

And through a storm of music whirl

   The dizzy waltz at Meyringen.


And they may sing, as oft they will,

   Of joy beneath the southern vine,

And in luxurious banquets fill

   Their goblets with the orient wine :—

But when the Alpland winter rolls

   His tempests over hill and glen,

Let me sit mid the steaming bowls

   That cheer the nights at Meyringen.


Brave men are there with hands adroit

   At every game our land deems good,—

To wrestle, or to swing the quoit,

   Or drain the bowl of brotherhood :—

And when the last wild chase is through,

We'll sit together, gray-haired men,

And, with the gay Lisette to brew,

Once more be young in Meyringen.

# THE WARNING.

THE song was done; they raised their eyes,
And saw between them and the skies
A figure standing dark and mute
  That on a gleaming rifle leant,
And all his form from head to foot
  Was painted on the firmament.
So still he stood, the quickest eye
In its first gazing toward the sky
Glanced twice, before discerning if
The dusky shape were man or cliff.

At length, a voice—so high and loud

It seemed descending from the cloud—

Swept down along the swelling gale,

And made the stoutest hearer quail.

"I charge ye, on!  I charge ye, speed!

And every gust proclaims the need.

By all the surest mountain signs,

By all the wailing of the winds,—

And by the sobbing of the pines,—

And by that avalanche which now

Gives warning through the vale below,—

By yonder rising cloud, whose wrath

Makes desperate the safest path,

I know the blast must soon perform

The bidding of the monarch storm."

# STORM ON ST. BERNARD.

Oh, Heaven, it is a fearful thing
Beneath the tempest's beating wing
To struggle, like a stricken hare
When swoops the monarch bird of air;
To breast the loud winds' fitful spasms,
To brave the cloud and shun the chasms,
Tossed like a fretted shallop-sail
Between the ocean and the gale.

Along the valley, loud and fleet,
The rising tempest leapt and roared,

And scaled the Alp, till from his seat

   The throned Eternity of Snow

His frequent avalanches poured

   In thunder to the storm below.


The laden tempest wildly broke

   O'er roaring chasms and rattling cliffs,

   And on the pathway piled the drifts;

   And every gust was like a wolf,—

And there was one at every cloak,—

   That, snarling, dragged toward the gulf.

The staggering mule scarce kept his pace,

   With ears thrown back and shoulders bowed;

The surest guide could barely trace

   The difference 'twixt earth and cloud;

And every form, from foot to face,

   Was in a winding-sheet of snow:

   The wind, 'twas like the voice of wo

That howled above their burial-place!

And now, to crown their fears, a roar
Like ocean battling with the shore,
Or like that sound which night and day
Breaks through Niagara's veil of spray,
From some great height within the cloud,
　To some immeasured valley driven,
Swept down, and with a voice so loud
　It seemed as it would shatter heaven!
The bravest quailed; it swept so near,
　It made the ruddiest cheek to blanch,
While look replied to look in fear,
　"The avalanche!　The avalanche!"
It forced the foremost to recoil,
　Before its sideward billows thrown,—
Who cried, "O God!　Here ends our toil!
　The path is overswept and gone!"


The night came down.　The ghostly dark,
　Made ghostlier by its sheet of snow,
　Wailed round them its tempestuous wo,

Like Death's announcing courier!  "Hark!
There, heard you not the alp-hound's bark?
And there again! and there!  Ah, no,
'Tis but the blast that mocks us so!"


Then through the thick and blackening mist
Death glared on them, and breathed so near,
    Some felt his breath grow almost warm,
The while he whispered in their ear
    Of sleep that should out-dream the storm.
Then lower drooped their lids,—when, "List!
Now, heard you not the storm-bell ring?
    And there again, and twice and thrice!
Ah, no, 'tis but the thundering
    Of tempests on a crag of ice!"


Death smiled on them, and it seemed good
    On such a mellow bed to lie:
The storm was like a lullaby,
And drowsy pleasure soothed their blood.

But still the sturdy, practised guide
His unremitting labour plied;
Now this one shook until he woke,
And closer wrapt the other's cloak,—
Still shouting with his utmost breath,
To startle back the hand of Death,
Brave words of cheer! —"But, hark again,—
Between the blasts the sound is plain;
The storm, inhaling, lulls,—and hark!
It is—it is! the alp-dog's bark!
And on the tempest's passing swell—
  The voice of cheer so long debarred—
There swings the Convent's guiding-bell,
  The sacred bell of Saint Bernard!"


Then how they gained, though chilled and faint,
  The Convent's hospitable door,
And breathed their blessing on the saint
  Who guards the traveller as of yore,—

Were long to tell:—And then the night
And unhoused winter of the height,
  Were rude for audience such as mine;
The harp, too, wakes to more delight,
The fingers take a freer flight,
  When warmed between the fire and wine.
The storm around the fount of song
Has blown its blast so chill and long,
What marvel if it freeze or fail,
Or that its spray returns in hail!
Or, rather, round my muse's wings
The encumbering snow, though melting, clings
So thickly, she can scarce do more
Than flounder where she most would soar.


The hand benumbed, reviving, stings,
And with thick touches only brings
  The harp-tones out by fits and spells,—
You needs must note how all the strings
  Together jar like icicles!

Then heap the hearth and spread the board,
And let the glowing flasks be poured,
While I beside the roaring fire
Melt out the music of my lyre.

# FANCIES IN THE FIRELIGHT,

## IN THE CONVENT OF ST. BERNARD.

Oh, it is a joy to gaze
Where the great logs lie ablaze;
Thus to list the garrulous flame
Muttering like some ancient dame;
And to hear the sap recount
Stories of its native mount,
Telling of the summer weather,
When the trees swayed all together,—

How the little birds would launch
Arrowy songs from branch to branch,
Till the leaves with pleasure glistened,
And each great bough hung and listened
To the song of thrush and linnet,
When securely lodged within it,
With all pleasant sounds that dally
Round the hill and in the valley;
Till each log and branch and splinter
On the ancient hearth of Winter
Can do naught but tell the story
Of its transient summer glory.

Oh, there's tranquil joy in gazing
Where these great logs lie ablazing,
While the wizard flame is sparkling,
The memorial shadows darkling
Swim the wall in strange mutation,
Till the marvelling contemplation

Feeds its wonder to repletion
With each firelight apparition.

There the ashen Alp appears,
And its glowing head uprears,
Like a warrior grim and bold,
With a helmet on of gold;
And a music goes and comes
Like the sound of distant drums.

O'er a line of serried lances
How the blazing banner dances,
While red pennons rise and fall
Over ancient Hannibal.

Lo, beneath a moon of fire,
Where the meteor sparks stream by her,
There I see the brotherhood
Which on sacred Grütli stood,

Pledging with crossed hands to stand
The defenders of the land.


And in that red ember fell
Gessler, with the dart of Tell!


Still they fall away, and, lo!
Other phantoms come and go,
Other banners wing the air,—
And the countless bayonets glare,
While around the steep way stir
Armies of the conqueror;
And the slow mule toiling on
Bears the world's Napoleon.


Now the transient flame that flashes
'Twixt the great logs and the ashes,
Sends a voice out from the middle
That my soul cannot unriddle,—

Till the fire above and under

Gnaws the stoutest wood asunder,

And the brands, in ruin blended,

Smoking, lie uncomprehended,—

While the dying embers blanch,

And the muffled avalanche,

Noiseless as the years descend,

Sweeps them to an ashen end.

Thus at last the great shall be,

   And the slave shall lie with them,—

*Pié Jesu Domine*

   *Dona eis requiem!*


END OF VOL. I.